Praise for the historical novels of Richard S. Wheeler:

The Buffalo Commons

"A taut drama about one of the most controversial issues in the modern West. [Wheeler] again demonstrates his story-telling genius in creating magnificent, believable characters. This is a fine novel and deserves a large readership. It is as timely as tomorrow's newspaper and once started, it is hard to put down. Wheeler has another award-winner on his hands."
—*Tulsa World*

"A strong novel." —*Seattle Post-Intelligencer*

"Wheeler has produced fiction, but the story deals with some very real issues. . . . By dramatizing and personalizing them, he makes them more real, more memorable, more significant."
—*The Sunday Oklahoman*

Rendezvous: A Barnaby Skye Novel

"An exciting story of a young man coming of age and growing into a reality greater than his dream."
—*Tulsa World*

"The Spur Award–winning Wheeler returns to good form with this adventure tale of his enduring frontier hero."
—*Publishers Weekly*

Continued . . .

THE
WITNESS

Richard S. Wheeler

A SIGNET BOOK

SIGNET
Published by New American Library, a division of
Penguin Putnam Inc., 375 Hudson Street,
New York, New York, 10014, U.S.A.
Penguin Books Ltd, 27 Wrights Lane,
London W8 5TZ, England
Penguin Books Australia Ltd, Ringwood,
Victoria, Australia
Penguin Books Canada Ltd, 10 Alcorn Avenue,
Toronto, Ontario, Canada M4V 3B2
Penguin Books (N.Z.) Ltd, 182–190 Wairau Road,
Auckland 10, New Zealand

Penguin Books Ltd, Registered Offices:
Harmondsworth, Middlesex, England

First published by Signet, an imprint of New American Library,
a division of Penguin Putnam Inc.

First Printing, July 2000
10 9 8 7 6 5 4 3 2 1

Prologue

I am going to tell you about heroes. Call me an observer. Call me a frontier philosopher. Call me a crank. Or call me Horatio Bates, if you prefer. Sure, that's a grandiose name to hang on a village postmaster, but my parents had designs upon my future that didn't include my becoming a minor government employee.

They had other things in mind, such as a professorship at Harvard, or a stint as secretary of state, or a career as the Edward Gibbon of the American republic, recording its history. I never spent a day in public school but was tutored so fiercely that by the age of eighteen I knew everything, or thought I did. Fortunately, about then, I grew weary of books and tutors and knowledge.

At that point, my ambitions and my parents' ambitions for me parted company. I headed west, full of adventure and armed with a sinecure as postmaster of a border town in Kansas. They grieved. I regretted disappointing them but was determined to make my own life.

Heavy responsibilities come with managing the posts. There is money in those envelopes, and love letters, and bills, and word from long-lost loved ones, and notices of death. But a postmaster is also the town sage and often an astute observer of the character of a town's inhabitants. Many's the time when I've been asked to recommend some citizen or other, and on occasion I have quietly declined.

And that brings me to my real vocation. Postmastering has never been anything more to me than a means to put bread on my table. I am a philosopher and scholar, probably no different from a thousand such village savants who dot the American landscape, save for the fact of my education.

My real vocation is the study of character. On the frontier, where I dwell, it is more visible and valuable than back in the settled areas of the country, which is why I drift from one border town to another, on the rim of settlement. I am endlessly fascinated with the way people conduct themselves under pressure. I tell myself that I am studying all this because I believe in a strong and virtuous nation. But that's just my rationale. I esteem moral courage for its own sake.

Show me an incorruptible man and I will write his name upon the sky. Show me a man who doesn't cave in to evil and I will exalt him above kings and presidents and popes. Show me a man of moral courage and I will shout his name from the mountaintops and preserve it for posterity, so that a hundred generations of Americans will know and revere his greatness.

I honor an incorruptible man for his own sake and have made a lifework of collecting stories about such people. That's why you may call me the Observer if you choose. I have recently taken to scribbling these stories for posterity. You will see me in many of them, playing some minor role or other, sometimes being nothing more than a listener or a counselor. And you will discover that I am a rootless man; every little while I hie myself to a new frontier town after arranging a transfer with my superiors in Washington. They gladly send me along—good frontier postmasters are hard to find.

Now, after years of collecting stories, I am ready to publish my findings. What I have in my collection is nothing less than heroic conduct by all sorts of people. They have surprised me, these people. Sometimes the timorous soul I would least expect to show some backbone turns out to be the only man in town willing to stand up for what is right and good. And sometimes the reverse is true; the man most versed in moral niceties is the man who fails under pressure.

I have seen great things, awesome courage, amazing strength under pressure, and I delight in telling you about them. These stories will lift your spirits and make you proud as punch to be an American. I will light bonfires on the mesas, compose songs, carve in granite the names of the anointed. I will show you what it means to be a man or woman of honor. Such people are the stuff of ballads, the soul of legends.

My job at the mail window is well nigh perfect for this odd vocation. Everyone in town eventually picks up mail, buys stamps, and visits with me. And it is a postmaster's luck—or curse—that some also confide in me, so that I know what lies in the souls of half the denizens of one of these frontier towns.

That's all you really need to know about old Bates. You'll find me wandering through these little yarns, and maybe even drawing some conclusions at the end. For I am the Observer.

Chapter 1

There it was! Daniel Knott, bookkeeper for the Merchant Bank of Paradise, spotted the entry in the ledger and knew the little mystery had been solved. He felt exceedingly pleased, not just because he had figured out a curious transaction, but because the discovery made him proud, oh, so proud, to be employed by such a noble man as Amos C. Burch.

Knott was aglow. Once again, Amos Burch had shown himself to be a generous and compassionate man, worthy of the high esteem he had garnered in Paradise, Colorado. Mr. Burch had spared the widow the foreclosure, and that kindness would rest well with the citizens of the town.

Knott enjoyed his detective skills. Little did people realize how much of their private life was bared to the eyes of a good accountant and teller. He figured he knew more about the lives of those in Paradise than anyone else in town.

Just yesterday, Mr. Burch had departed by buggy for the ranch of the widow, Eloise Joiner, about five miles up the valley. His purpose, he explained to Knott, was to break the bad news to Mrs. Joiner. She was four months in arrears on her January 1 mortgage payment and owed the bank $571, the amount overdue on a balance of $2,200. There was no way out but for the bank to foreclose.

"After all, Daniel," Burch had said, "it's not the bank's money. It's the depositors' funds that we've loaned, and we must protect our depositors at all costs."

Knott had heard that idea from the first day he had been employed at Burch's bank, six years earlier. It was sound banking practice. A bank had the obligation and duty to protect the hard-won assets of its customers.

But when Burch returned, he said no more about the foreclosure, and Knott chewed on that in his mind. Then he discovered a $600 deposit in the widow's account, and a $571 withdrawal obviously intended to make the mortgage current, and the payment recorded on the mortgage ledger. But where had the $600 come from? Ah, that was the mystery.

Mrs. Joiner's husband, Rolf, had died the year before, and she had struggled on alone, her sole son long gone and living in California. She had rented the pastures, hoping to make ends meet that way, but the tenants had been careless and improvident—Knott could have told her that, but there was just so much a teller could say—and had paid her very little. And so the lovely Eloise had slipped farther and farther behind. But a certain someone had deposited enough in her account to stave off disaster.

A comely woman, Mrs. Joiner. About forty, Knott estimated, with a crown of black hair, a knowing smile, and the vibrant features and form of a much younger woman. It surprised him that she had not remarried. But that, too, was not his business. She had every right to be particular.

And just now, he had bared the secret. The funds had come from Amos Burch himself. There indeed was the withdrawal from Burch's own account and the posting in Mrs. Joiner's. Ah! So some small tragedy had been averted that day. With typical modesty, Burch had posted the transaction in the great, gray buckram-bound ledger himself, not wanting his charity to be obvious to his staff. Mr. Knott's joy bloomed at the thought. Amos Burch was a sensitive gentleman.

Done with his toil for the day, Knott turned down the lamp wick and closed the books, knowing everything was in perfect balance. Twilight was descending, and soon the mountain-girt town of Paradise would see the first stars emerge in the clear, quiet air. He could think of no more perfect place on earth than the aptly named Paradise. This was where he was bringing up his family, where he and his wife had put down deep roots and won the esteem of the community. This was a town with a future, a town with broad avenues, spacious white clapboard homes, and a bustling red-brick business district.

Paradise was quietly guided by Amos Burch, and every citizen had benefited because of it. Mr. Burch actually owned much of the county. He possessed several large ranches, Rand's Mercantile, the Clarion Hotel, two stagecoach lines, the water company, the Sally Mine with its rich silver lode, a cordwood dealership, Beck's Creamery, the Harvest Bakery, Colorado Livery Stable, and numerous lots and tracts. If his hand had rested heavily on Paradise, people might have felt differently about him. But in fact, Knott had never heard a harsh word about his employer.

It was true, of course, that a word from Burch was all it took to elect the judge, sheriff, county commissioners, clerk of court, mayor, councilmen, and other officers of the town and county. It was true that every citizen did business with him—if not at the bank, then in his numerous stores and enterprises. But here, too, his hand rested lightly on Paradise. He did not gouge customers, and he went out of his way to make sure everyone was happy.

His charities were legendary. Not an impoverished soul failed to receive a Christmas basket, and those who confronted medical ailments or other disasters found a bundle of cash in an unmarked envelope at their door. Everyone knew that such succor came from Burch, but he never revealed himself.

Nor was that the end of it. He had an amiable and affectionate wife, Myrtle, and adult children who seemed unaware that they were members of the most prominent family in town. The citizens of Paradise would gladly have sent him to the White House if they had had the power to do so. Under such leadership Paradise had prospered and bloomed, and no one was left behind.

Knott contemplated all that as he stored the ledger, locked $496.23 in the black safe, turned the battered sign on the bank door to Closed, and donned his old alpaca coat against a stiff April chill. Lamplight glowed from Burch's door, and Knott decided to let Mr. Burch know—very privately, of course—how pleased he was at this new largesse.

He rapped lightly and entered, as he always did, finding Burch totaling his own accounts at his massive oak desk. Burch's office was not grand, but it was tastefully appointed and very much attuned to the man who possessed it. Burch's wealth was discreet wealth.

"I'm going now, Mr. Burch. You'll lock up?"

"Yes, surely, Daniel."

"I want to say, sir—I'm glad it wasn't necessary to foreclose on Mrs. Joiner."

Burch smiled. The bank president had a high forehead, graying hair, extravagant muttonchops, a curiously formed broken nose that suggested a collision with a traveling fist, and a mild-mannered gaze that suggested acceptance of those in his presence. He radiated will and intelligence, and something else—respect for the ancient virtues.

"We won't say anything, will we, Daniel?"

"No, sir. But I personally wanted to thank you. Those were your personal funds—"

"Ah, you bookkeepers! A man has no secrets."

"Well, I just think it was a noble thing to do. I suppose Mrs. Joiner was most appreciative—"

"Ah, indeed, but I want your word, Daniel. Not a whisper of this to anyone. Not your wife, not a soul, right?"

"You are a modest man, Mr. Burch. This should be celebrated by all of Paradise."

"No!"

The sharpness in his voice startled Knott. He had scarcely ever heard a forceful word from Burch.

"No, Daniel. You will keep this secret. You will reveal it at your peril."

Knott stared at a new man. This Burch was not mild of eye, and his tone was not benign.

"Yes, sir," he said. "As the Bible says, 'In matters of charity the right hand should not know what the left hand is doing.'"

Burch's imperial glare swiftly vanished. "All right, then, Daniel. You're my right-hand man, and you do . . . not . . . know what the left is doing."

He waved Knott out of the room.

The bookkeeper braved the night air, hiking along Cedar Street, the town's main thoroughfare, past the county courthouse square. He trudged past a block containing a drygoods store, two hotels, a harness shop, blacksmith, bakery, butcher, hardware, law offices, and a greengrocer. He passed the Sweetwater Saloon, the only one in town, and one of Burch's properties. In the Sweetwater bartenders willingly served two or three beers, or one or two spirituous drinks, but then discouraged additional sales. Though Burch's hand rested lightly, it did shape the mores of the citizens, and Knott had heard of occasions when undesirables had been quietly advised to leave town. Drunks were not tolerated in Paradise.

Knott turned left on Juniper Street and walked contentedly toward his own white frame house, with its white picket fence and spacious lot. Lamplight glowed in the windows. He knew every one of his neighbors for two blocks in either direction. This was an orderly world, safe as mankind could make it. Four blocks north, the street petered out into a grassy hillside, and beyond that lay a vast and lawless hinterland rising toward the snowy San Juans in the distance. He could not imagine a more sublime, secure, or beautiful place on earth. Here, in a new land, was a city stretching its hands upward toward heaven.

He sometimes asked himself how he could be so lucky, and in those moments his thoughts always returned to one vital thing: he considered himself, like his employer, a man of integrity. Each day he handled hundreds, even thousands, of dollars. Each day he made sure that every cent was accounted for. If so much as a penny was missing, he would replace it with one from his own pocket. One time, when seven dollars had mysteriously vanished and could not be found in the cash drawers or books,

Knott had quietly placed seven dollars from his own purse in the cash drawer. That was two days' wages. He earned a hundred dollars a month, which made him one of the better-paid citizens of Paradise.

That integrity was the secret. He was trusted by Mr. Burch, by his neighbors, by his friends and family, by merchants, by ranchers and mine managers and teamsters, and by little children who put their pennies into their own savings accounts to get 2 percent interest. Virtue was its own reward, but it had wrought most of the joys of his life.

Knott's pace quickened with the thought of his wife and children in the house just ahead. He was a lucky man, and he knew why.

When he opened the gate in his picket fence, Rascal greeted him, the mongrel's tail wagging the whole mutt. He could always count on that greeting; within the house his evening arrival evoked differing responses. Hannah could be aglow when he stepped in and kissed her cheek, or she could ignore him. Sometimes the children rushed to greet him; more often they didn't. He understood. Life was not smooth. Sometimes he left his wicket at the bank feeling irritable. Sometimes Hannah was weary from her endless chores, or nursing a migraine, or fuming at the children. Peter could be sullen and silent, except when talking about horses. Rosalie, the youngest, would simply ignore her father. She was at an age when mere fathers didn't exist. And Daniel Junior sometimes stared at his father, obviously weighing whether fathers were useful commodities, more valuable than a baseball mitt.

He understood all that. Not even Paradise could make life go smoothly.

But this evening everything was fine. Hannah smiled as she whipped butter into the mashed potatoes.

"You had a good day. I can tell," she said.

"Yes, I did. I was inspired by something I discovered today, and I've felt good ever since."

"That's what you should say to me when you learn I'm expecting."

He gaped. "Good God, Hannah!"

She laughed. "I'm not expecting. But that's what you should say. Women like compliments."

He knew that later on she was going to tease him about the look on his face, and he would laugh with her. Children were welcome in Paradise, Colorado.

Chapter 2

Amos C. Burch knew himself to be an honorable man, and that was what was deviling him as he steered his lacquered ebony barouche around the quagmires of the Alamosa road.

He could not and would not turn back now. He had not known what paradise was until recently, but now he knew. True paradise was breathtaking, but it had complicated his life. He loved simplicity in all his affairs. Simplicity in business. Simplicity in theology. Simplicity in domestic life. Even simplicity in name. His middle name was Cash, and he wished it had been his surname, so that his initials would be ABC instead of ACB.

His powerful jet-haired gelding, El Morocco, drew the carriage easily through the springtime slop. In recent weeks the horse had enjoyed a dozen outings, each of them along the same road up the valley, each ending at the modest shake-roofed

board-and-batten ranch house owned by Eloise
Joiner—and of late, the Merchant Bank of Paradise.

Of these frequent spring jaunts he had said almost nothing to his employees. Once he announced
that he was looking at ranch properties, a perfect
truth beyond reproach. On one other occasion he
had announced to Knott that he was going out to
counsel Mrs. Joiner on the management of her
spread because the woman was not gifted in such
matters.

That, too, was a truth beyond cavil. She had
leased her pastures to the Jaekels, narrow-eyed,
low-browed father and son bachelor neighbors,
who were systematically mulcting her of grass,
cooking the books, and paying her a quarter of what
they ought to be. Burch considered it a duty to en-
lighten Eloise about matters once handled expertly
by her late husband. She was an apt student, eager
to learn everything—indeed, everything—that he
could teach her.

Amos Burch counted himself a successful man,
and knew it had little to do with luck. His flair for
business had been built upon the simplest of all pre-
cepts: keep customers happy. He did not regard his
customers as cows to be milked, nor did he try to
squeeze the last cent out of a transaction. Quite the
contrary. The various managers of his enterprises
had been carefully trained to be accommodating
and helpful to everyone. It had paid off. He was
rich. He more or less owned Archuleta County and
controlled its destiny. He owned the courthouse and

city hall too. He owned nearly everything that mattered, including the weekly paper, the *Paradise Tattler*. His empire ought to last for generations if his heirs followed the Amos Cash Burch golden rule: Keep 'em all happy.

He had heard himself extolled from the pulpits of the four churches in Paradise, and it didn't surprise him. Scarcely a meeting of the county commissioners or a session of the city council passed without an amiable reference to him. He routinely received offers to be the marshal of a parade, or to give the keynote address at a political rally, or to speak to students at commencement ceremonies, or to lead the community at prayer breakfasts, or to be the lay reader at the joint Thanksgiving Day service.

He belonged to all the fraternal organizations as a matter of course, and quietly contributed to their good works. Did the Kiwanis wish to raise funds for some Christmas charities? See Amos. Did the Odd Fellows pine to launch a scholarship to send a student from Paradise to college? See Amos. Did the Benevolent and Protective Order of the Elks hanker to install benches in the courthouse square? See Amos.

Did a widow whose mortgage payment failed to arrive at the Merchant Bank have any recourse? See Amos.

The thought sent a certain electric charge through his lean body. He was forty-six, not exactly a handsome man, but nonetheless possessing a presence. That's really what he liked to be among others; a presence. And given his health and virility and the good life he was living, he expected to be a presence for thirty years more.

Myrtle would not approve of these trips, but that could not be helped. Myrtle had everything except health. She lived in the finest and most elegantly appointed house in town, copied after an antebellum plantation mansion. She was the first lady of Paradise. She had raised two boisterous sons, who were nonetheless mannered when a quiet word was spoken to them. One had gone to normal school to become a Latin teacher. The other was touring Wales and Cornwall to broaden himself. She had position and handsomeness and a devoted husband . . .

That's where his thoughts tripped for the smallest second, like the slightest stumble of his dray horse. Myrtle would not know, so there was nothing to disapprove of. But it still bothered him. He was not simply an honorable man, but an enlightened one as well. He thought of others, after all.

Eloise Joiner stirred fires in him he never knew he possessed, fires never awakened in all his intimate years with Myrtle. It had been unplanned; his intentions innocent and pure. At least that is what he told himself. But he wondered now what subterranean fires had smoldered for years within him.

It was a grand day to be out. The spring sun blessed the land and tossed its light into the budding trees and onto the grassy hills. El Morocco pranced cheerfully along the rutted road. He passed the ranches of people he knew; the Byrds, the

Maples, the Koviches, and came at last to the two
ruts across verdant hills that led to the Joiner ranch.
It wasn't a large spread, but suitably managed, it
could yield a comfortable income in good times.
And who could ever say what would happen in bad
times?

She was waiting on the shaded porch.

The first time he had come, weeks earlier, she
wasn't expecting him, and she swiftly wiped her
hands—she had been scrubbing the kitchen floor—
to greet him. He remembered it all like a bright re-
curring dream.

He told her why he had come. She had wept. She
seemed to wilt, and he held her up, but then something happened that he would never forget. By
some mysterious alchemy, the moment was trans-
muted into something entirely different. She didn't
pull away, nor did he release her. That was how it
began. Since then, he had found all sorts of reasons
to visit her, and she welcomed him. Once or twice
he had carefully lured her to Paradise where they
arranged to have "accidental" meetings and visit.
He loved the innocence in her eyes, the lascivious-
ness of her lips, her tall figure as well as her imperial
posture.

He had swiftly taken care of the delinquency. He
had ousted the miserable, scowling, cheating
Jaekels from her property and arranged for Gordy
Drinnan, one of his own ranch managers, to lease
the land for a generous sum and stock it. The Jaekels
had threatened him, and now found themselves in

various property tax troubles. A soft word at the courthouse had done it. His own sturdy Herefords dotted the verdant slopes of the Joiner ranch. What could be more natural than checking on his cattle now and then?

She was no longer desperate. The arrangement pleased Amos C. Burch mightily. Life would continue just as it had. Myrtle would remain his beloved wife. His sons would never hear a whisper.

They had created a simple schedule: a late lunch on Tuesdays and Fridays, at which she always greeted him dressed in her handsomest frocks, followed by a sun-drenched, leisurely, exotic, and utterly delightful afternoon with a breathtaking great-souled woman, all alone in a hushed ranch house.

"Amos, love," she said as he approached, having run his dray horse and barouche into the barn aisle to keep the beast out of the sun—or so he told himself.

Her kiss was ample and happy and very experienced.

"I wish you would come here every day. I can hardly bear the long silences without you," she whispered as he held her tight. "You lift me so high."

"And you, my dear, are cherubim and seraphim, and all the powers and principalities of heaven," he replied.

"Someday," she whispered, "someday I hope you can find a way . . ."

He smiled but said nothing, wanting to discourage that sort of talk.

"I don't know how long I can bear this," she said. "Please find a way, Amos."

"I can't promise you anything, Eloise," he said.

She nodded.

He would always have to be firm. No divorce, no scandal, no change in the outward rhythms of his life. From the beginning she had spoken of marriage. She had expressed the belief that this period was a secret engagement, not a liaison. She had told him she wanted always to hold her head high, go to church without being singed by her conscience, and express her love openly and joyously.

That had been a problem, but not beyond the considerable resources of Amos C. Burch. Money was the stairway to heaven. That and vague promises, glowing, hazy, and ultimately noncommittal.

"Ah, Eloise, you are the fairest rose in Paradise," he said.

She laughed. "You'd say anything."

She had a way of deflating his sentiments that he rather liked. It made her earthy and supplied humor to their memorable afternoons.

He knew, as he feasted on her cinnamon-spiced apple pie, that he would have to stay one jump ahead of her, that she would soon grow restless and he would need to enmesh her even more in security, savings, comforts. And he knew, too, that ultimately a lady of her quality would end the liaison because she had to in order to preserve her soul. Burch was not an unsophisticated man, especially when it came to women.

He loved Myrtle, who had soldiered along the path with him. He had been a man of modest means when they married, back East. Many years elapsed before he was able to shower her with everything her heart desired. They had been through tribulations together. Scarlet fever had almost killed Danny. Dilworth, named after Myrtle's family, had been caught by the Lincoln School principal tampering with a girl in a lavatory. Though it had been hushed up, Dilworth had been severely reprimanded and warned that any further offense would send him to boarding school in Connecticut.

That was all part of life, and Amos Burch accepted it. He would keep Myrtle happy. She didn't much care anymore for the intimate bliss of marriage, and that now suited him fine. Amos Burch, first citizen of Paradise, had another and infinitely richer source of bliss.

Chapter 3

Little did Daniel Knott know what fate would deal him that languid June evening in Paradise. The summer sun lingered late, gilding the stately cotton-woods and highlighting the westerly slopes of the mountains. It was a Wednesday. Families had completed their chores and now lounged amicably on the spacious verandas and porches that dotted the town.

Knott had a small task to complete at the bank and left Hannah and the children to enjoy the soft evening and the crawling purple shadows when the sun fell behind the San Juan Mountains. He hastened along Cedar Street and turned toward the bank, wanting to make short work of the task.

On Friday the semiannual report was due. Twice a year he summed the accounts, noted which loans and mortgages were performing and which weren't, and compared balances and assets with those of the previous period, putting all of this into terse and readable prose for the bank's directors, chief of which was its president and chairman, Amos C. Burch.

There was scarcely a buggy or horse in the business district, except for a few saddlers at the saloon hitching rail. Who in his right mind would be in town when the whole sweet outdoors beckoned so seductively? Knott himself wished he might avoid the task at hand, but by day he was too busy at the teller window to put his report together.

He let himself in through the bank's rear door but did not light a lamp. That was the moment when he saw a thin bar of light under the closed door of Amos Burch's office. That surprised Knott. When did Burch ever spend an evening at the Merchant Bank of Paradise?

"Amos!" he said, knocking once and opening the door, as he usually did.

He would never forget what he saw in those few ticks of the clock, the two of them there on the horsehair sofa, as startled as Knott, like red-eyed deer in lantern light. Hastily he slammed the door shut, his pulse climbing, the wind knocked out of him by some giant, invisible fist. It was as if lightning had suddenly exposed, in its blinding blue brilliance, the darkest secret of Paradise.

He knew at once that Burch's gift to Eloise Joiner had not been charity, nor had charity inspired the leasing of Mrs. Joiner's ranch to Burch. He knew that nothing in Paradise was as it had always seemed, and that Amos C. Burch was not the man he had supposed, in his innocence, to be the very soul of rectitude and benevolence.

No!

Half-witted with shock, Knott thought for a moment of going to his desk and beginning work on his report, but then he dismissed that notion as madness. He bolted from the bank, making a great noise in the closing and locking of doors, and fled down the street toward his white home, fleeing from the vision scorched into his brain in the ticking clockwork of revelation.

"Daniel," Hannah said, "you're back so soon."

"Yes," he said, pausing on the veranda.

"What's wrong? Something's wrong."

Knott decided then and there to say not a word, not now, not ever, not to anyone, including his wife.

"Nothing. I didn't feel like working."

"Are you ill?"

"Nothing!" It was all but a shout.

Hannah eyed him unhappily, caught his hand for a moment, squeezed it, and walked into the darkened house. Knott stumbled into a wicker chair, which groaned under his sudden weight. He spent the rest of the evening alone, staring into the gathering dusk, watching the small blue band of light over the San Juans diminish and fade to nothing until only the glittering stars remained to light the heavens.

Amos and Eloise.

He did not know how he could report for work

the next day. He even weighed the question of re-signing. And if he did report, he didn't know how he could look Amos Burch in the face.

Later, in bed, Hannah whispered to him. "I know something's wrong, Daniel. If I've done something wrong, tell me. I'm sorry if I have."

"It's just bank problems," he said.

"It's more than that," she said. "I guess you'll tell me when you're ready. But I'm feeling left out."

He did not sleep.

But the next day proceeded normally. He arrived promptly at eight, as usual, after a brisk walk through fresh air, and let himself in the rear door. He opened the safe, counted out the cash for the tellers' trays, welcomed his two colleagues, Jasper Pickering and Miss Gustafson, and unlocked the double front doors at nine. It proved to be a sleepy Thursday, like so many other Thursdays.

"Miss Gustafson, you look ravishing today," he said.

She dimpled up. "You say that every day, Daniel."

"Yes, but it's true."

"If you say it too much, the coinage will cheapen."

He smiled. Not many people complimented Miss Gustafson, which is one reason he liked to. She rarely smiled.

Burch showed up about ten, and Knott spiraled through some nervous moments. But Burch confined himself to his commodious offices at the rear of the building.

Not until Knott locked the doors at three, posting the Closed sign and beginning to sum up the accounts in the buckram-bound ledgers, did matters change.

"Daniel, I wish to see you," Burch said.

Knott hurried into Burch's office, choked with such anxiety that he could scarcely keep his lunch down.

Burch looked pleasant enough, and eyed Knott with that famous gaze that seemed to peer straight through a man. "Close the door, please," he said.

That's when Knott knew he was in trouble. His hands dripped sweat.

"You've been a fine bookkeeper and teller, Daniel," Burch began smoothly.

"Thank you, sir."

"I'm going to promote you."

That was the last thing Daniel Knott had expected. He registered Burch's words with some difficulty.

"Have a seat, for heaven's sake. Don't stand there like some lackey. I'm making you the vice president and cashier of the Merchant Bank, and raising your salary to three hundred a month. You'll act as my surrogate, and I am going to turn over to you the day-to-day operations of the bank. I plan to devote more time to other enterprises. Congratulations, Daniel. You've earned it."

"Earned it?"

"Of course! You're my senior man. You've managed the place for two years and scarcely realized it. About all I do these days is approve loans. You're fully capable of that."

Knott scarcely knew what to make of it. But he knew one thing for certain: this was not really about his abilities, and it wasn't an ordinary promotion.

"Ah . . . thank you, sir."

"You are now, Daniel, the best-paid salaried man in the county. I know that for a fact. Your annual income is now among the top half-dozen incomes in the county. It's a laurel wreath on your head. The bank and its directors will be entirely comfortable with you at the helm."

"Well—thank you, sir. I didn't expect . . . this is a surprise."

"It shouldn't be." Burch smiled and extended a dry, smooth hand. Knott shook it with his clammy one, his mind a jumble of conflicting feelings.

"Go take Hannah to dinner at the Log Cabin," Burch said. "Celebrate."

"Yes, yes, sir," Knott said, backing out and carefully closing the door behind him. The last thing he saw was the horsehair couch.

A cornucopia! He was suddenly flush. He had paid eighteen hundred dollars for his house. Now he was earning so much he could buy two houses a year. He could pay off his mortgage. He could send his children to college and scarcely sacrifice to do it. He and Hannah could take a long trip somewhere, by rail and steamer, and he would not need to sweat out the payments for it.

He could purchase securities: railroad stocks, bonds, even land, and build up some retirement funds. In the blink of an eye he had gone from being a low-level bank employee to a man of substance. He would be numbered among the first men of Paradise.

He did the books, closed up, and headed out into the afternoon sun. The fresh, juniper-scented air rolling down from the San Juans reminded him that he lived in a larger universe, and that this universe—at least according to Daniel Knott's belief— was governed by immutable laws and principles.

He strolled slowly home, wondering what to say to Hannah. This was not just about his abilities. Amos Burch was purchasing something: silence, unquestioned loyalty, instant obedience. Amos Burch was burying a terrible secret with this astonishing promotion.

Knott agonized. He would enjoy the incredible raise. But he would be expected to keep the secret. He sensed, as he strolled home that summer afternoon, that he had only two choices: accept the raise and all it implied, or resign and leave town. He could see no middle ground. If he accepted that raise, he would be Burch's man. If he didn't, he would have a lot of explaining to do to Hannah and the children. Where would they go? He had no reserves. The family had consumed all he could bring home in the fortnightly brown pay envelopes.

At least he could take some time to think things through. Burch had simply assumed he would accept the raise, and that was that.

Hannah wasn't home when he got there. He supposed she was shopping. No children greeted him, either, but that was normal. During the high, sweet days of summer, the children of Paradise fished the river, hiked the hills, raced their ponies over wild land, built tree houses.

Until that day, his whitewashed house, secure and sunny, had been his refuge. He paced through it now, room by room. The dining room, where Hannah nurtured her children while teaching them manners. The living room, where he read the *Rocky Mountain News* and she darned stockings and sewed shirts by the light of the kerosene lamps. The larger bedroom, the children's rooms. The well in back, where the family jacked buckets of water with a vigorous pumping of the black iron handle. The little carriage barn, where they kept the old buggy. The garden, where they nursed lettuce and tomatoes and potatoes and fought beetles. The privy, always in need of lime.

It had seemed so solid, so secure. Now it seemed fragile and imperiled.

He didn't know what to do, and he couldn't even discuss his dilemma with Hannah. Maybe that was the worst of it: if he accepted, he would forever wall off a secret from his own dear wife.

Chapter 4

Hannah arrived home bearing a basket of fresh peas, and Rosalie was toting a crock of butter.

"Daniel," she said, her eyes welcoming him. She poured the pea pods into a colander.

Rosalie opened the ice chest and stuffed the butter into it, dimpled up a big smile for her father, and then retreated into the lush outdoors.

"Hannah! I've been promoted."

It had simply erupted from him, scattering all his resolves like marbles across a floor. Thus, in the smallest fraction of a second, he had sealed his fate.

"Daniel! A raise?"

He closed his eyes a moment, wanting to feel a flood of joy, but feeling only dread. "Yes. I've been made vice president and cashier. I'm going to be running the bank most of the time. And I'll be earning three hundred a month."

"Three hundred?"

She gazed at him, dumbstruck.

"Mr. Burch said I would be the highest-paid salary man in Paradise. A few earn more, but they aren't salaried."

She set down her colander, wiped her hands on a kitchen towel, and led him to the parlor.

"Tell me everything. Every word he said," she whispered.

Knott fought back a drowning sensation. He no longer had any options. So he told her how he had been invited into Burch's office late in the afternoon, commended, and then given the raise and the new responsibilities.

"We will be comfortable now," he said.

She kissed him gently there on the sofa, and then stared. "Something is wrong," she said.

He nodded. "I'm not sure this has anything to do with my merits."

"What, then, Daniel?"

"I—can't say. Maybe I'm just imagining things."

"You're keeping something from me. I guess you will if you must. Business is like that, I guess. Especially bank business. Banks keep little secrets in their lockboxes."

He nodded unhappily. He wanted the whole truth to rush out, everything he knew. But the words died in his throat. "We'll put money by. We'll save something for the children."

"You aren't very happy," she said. "I don't understand."

"Mr. Burch said I should take you to the Log Cabin as a celebration."

She shook her head. "I've got fresh peas and there's a rhubarb pie in the safe, and cold ham and potato salad—"

"Some other time, then. I like your food better than the Log Cabin's."

"I can keep a secret," she said, inviting him to talk.

"That's what Amos Burch wants me to do. Keep a secret."

She sat, her hands tugging at the folds of her skirt, and then she rose. "I will never ask you what," she said. "It must be awfully important. Amos Burch is a good man."

She drifted back to the kitchen, and Knott sensed that a small, cruel wedge had been driven between him and his wife that hour.

He heard Hannah calling out the back door for Rosalie to come in and set the table. Maybe tonight, alone, after the children were abed, he would tell Hannah the whole terrible story. Maybe she would understand. Maybe she would agree to move away from Paradise.

But that was like Adam asking Eve to leave Eden.

He didn't sleep well that night. Twice he arose, prowling the shadowy house, so burdened that it felt like something was crushing the air out of his lungs. And yet nothing seemed amiss.

Hannah greeted him with a warm hand after the

second of these wanderings. "If you don't want to accept the raise, Daniel, I'll try to understand."

"There is no other woman like you," he replied.

"No advancement is worth it if it torments you."

"I can't just turn it down, Hannah."

"But why?"

"I just can't."

He felt the invisible canyon between them widening again.

She turned her back to him and pretended to sleep, and so the night passed.

The next day proceeded smoothly. Promptly at nine, Knott unlocked the double doors, and went about his ordinary business at his teller's wicket. But the bank seemed different, if only in his mind. It had always seemed the very Gibraltar of Paradise, the place where a thousand dreams were stored in ledgers, the place where stories unfolded—dwindling sums suggesting a business was in trouble, mounting balances suggesting that a rancher or a dairyman or a blacksmith was prospering. Everything was the same as before. Just the same.

He closed the doors at three, as usual, and he and his colleagues began the daily task of totaling up the ledgers and making sure everything balanced.

Knott wasn't surprised when Burch once again invited him into his sanctum, meeting him with a genial smile.

"Well, Daniel, did your wife enjoy dining out?"

"We didn't go, sir. She had dinner ready."

"How did she take the news, eh?"

"She said you're a noble man, sir. But we're both a bit puzzled."

"Ah, no need to be. I'm very content. I take it that the new arrangement is entirely satisfactory?"

This time Knott found himself the recipient of a steady, unblinking gaze that was not wallpapered by geniality.

"I was thinking, sir, that this is a bit hasty. I'm not sure I'm ready for these responsibilities. Maybe in a year. I wish to learn more about management, about loans . . ." The words sputtered out and died.

"Daniel, I don't make offers lightly. Take the promotion or leave my employ. I don't want someone who is indecisive."

There it was. Knott had foreseen it: Burch would own his unquestioning loyalty—or put him out of work. Knott knew that a word from Burch would keep anyone else in town from hiring him.

"Yes, sir, I accept. I will do the best I can for the bank."

"For me. The bank is really mine, Daniel. Frankly, the directors are furniture."

"For you, sir."

"Very well. Your raise begins with the next pay period. You will, of course, have this office soon. I'm going to remodel upstairs and run my various businesses from there. I'll wall off the stairs and have my own entrance."

"It'll be strange, sitting in that chair, sir."

Burch smiled. "I imagine you'll get used to it

quickly enough. Your first task will be to hire someone to replace you."

"You want me to choose?"

"It's all your responsibility now, Daniel. The
bank's in your hands."

"I am honored by your confidence in me, sir."

Burch nodded and smiled.

During the next days, carpenters and joiners
swarmed through the brick building, and Daniel
heard a great deal of hammering and sawing upstairs. Occasionally he drifted up there to watch the
progress, and he soon discovered that Burch's new
lair was not merely a comfortable office but a small
suite, with a parlor, a miniature kitchen, and a bedroom alcove.

When Burch did things, he did them with all the
force of an avalanche. Wainscoting, red-flocked
wallpaper, brass chandeliers with coal-oil lamps, a
silk divan, a walnut desk . . . even a four-poster
with mosquito netting.

Knott put a Help Wanted sign in the bank window and a small ad in the *Tattler*, and began inter-
viewing candidates for the teller job. The bank ran
smoothly. When lines formed at the teller windows,
Knott pitched in and made transactions just as he
had done before. It was going to be fine.

Most of the candidates faltered when he put their
mathematics to the test. But finally a widow woman
he knew well, Adah Wainwright, who supported
herself with rentals, applied, sailed through the ad-
dition, subtraction, multiplication, and division,

and showed herself to be a master of the ledgers. He employed her, knowing full well that she was the first woman in Paradise to hold such a position.

But Knott didn't worry about that. He elevated Pickering to chief teller, while Miss Gustafson continued to clerk and take dictation. He purchased an ad in the *Tattler* announcing the personnel changes and plunged into his work with gusto. With every hour he spent in that commodious office chair that had once supported Burch's ample bottom, he gained confidence and courage. He listened to loan petitions from stockmen, teamsters, and dozens of others, including a young cowboy who wanted to speculate in blooded cattle.

Mostly he turned them down. And yet he had to put the money to use. If it did not draw interest, he would drive the Merchant Bank of Paradise into insolvency. He made his first loan to a stockman he knew well, Jason Albright. The credit would help Albright purchase two patented homesteads that would supply grass, some good springs, and shelter some of his ranch hands.

A month passed. Knott rarely saw Amos Burch and rarely even received instructions from his employer, although he knew he was being carefully monitored.

Burch was often out of Paradise, checking on properties. But now Knott sensed that he was doing more than assessing properties during his perambulations. If Burch was spending evenings in his upstairs lair, Knott didn't know of it—he made a point of leaving the bank before the supper hour and not returning until morning.

Hannah rejoiced in the new income. The Knotts indulged themselves for the first time in their lives. They received the congratulations of their neighbors. Daniel was strong-armed onto the boards of a dozen civic organizations, and he found the pace of his life quickening. He was even asked to address high school seniors about career choices, speak at fraternal picnics, recruit teachers for the schools, and spearhead the effort to bring a Denver and Rio Grande Railroad branch line to Paradise.

Everything was rosy, and nothing marred the cheerful passage of his life, and all was blue sky.

Chapter 5

Myrtle Burch tried hard to set aside her sorrows, but they stole through her no matter how resolutely she struggled to be happy. The arthritis in her hands, and now increasingly in her knees, had brutally circumscribed her life. She had loved to embroider and do crewelwork, but now she could bear only a few minutes of it before her gnarled hands began to torture her.

She might be the first lady of Archuleta County, with position and abundance her lot in life, but these things did not compensate her for the deepening sorrow that stained each hour of each day. What was position without love? What was abundance when she was starved for her husband's affection? What good was life when she was nothing but a castoff? Where had happiness fled?

She was a neglected woman. Years ago it had been a subtle thing, something she barely noticed in her busy rounds. She poured her energies into her household and her boys, and imagined that Amos's business was what kept him away from home or made him too tired to say much when he did return to the hearth. Men had their ways, and the wise woman made her own life and didn't worry about such things.

She never complained. She kept busy. When her arthritis had made housework difficult, Amos swiftly provided a housekeeper and part-time cook. And that, actually, had freed Myrtle to visit with friends, join other women in various clubs, such as her Great Books Society, and engage in more charity work.

At least Amos had come home in those days. Now he rarely did. He had turned the upstairs of the bank into his private suite, he said. She had never been up there, though she would have liked to see where he squandered so much of his time. She had asked once, but he said it was just a place of business consisting of an office and meeting rooms, with a small bedroom. She wondered why he needed that. The bank was only six blocks away.

Then things changed swiftly. Amos had turned over his banking duties to young Mr. Knott, elevating the man to a lofty position with great responsibility, and Myrtle thought that at last she would see more of Amos. But she was wrong. She saw even less of him. She heard that he was often out of town overseeing his ranches. Well, she could understand that. A man with Amos's responsibilities carried heavy burdens.

But somehow none of that rang true. Something was quite wrong. She hadn't the faintest idea what it might be. On the surface everything flowed along as before, but she knew it wasn't really so. Something had changed. Neglect had turned into something else. Amos paid the bills, stayed around the house on Sundays as if doing penance, and escorted her to stockgrowers' banquets and Sunday services. His politeness was suffocating. Fear lanced her. Amos had become a stranger, affable and genial and cordial, but beyond those eyes lay a private and very distant life.

She told herself she ought to be content. How many women who suffered such terrible arthritis could turn over every household chore, including laundering sheets and ironing shirts, to two domestics?

But the more she counted her blessings, the more desolate she became. At first, when her bones ached from the painful disease that was creeping through her body, she welcomed his indifference to her in their intimate life. His fitful bouts of lovemaking had stirred not passion but pain, but she had always tried to please him. And then it had all stopped, like a clock that no longer ticked. Amos Burch no longer fondled his wife. She feared that even more than the pain she experienced.

She could not say just when she *knew* he had a woman. But it had lodged in her mind, a quiet accusation, purely intuitive, without the slightest proof. She knew, but she didn't know how or why.

That is how she thought of it, her mind feathering about the topic, her thoughts avoiding certain words and phrases, ever proper, ever delicate, ever careful of her own sensibilities. She simply feather-dusted the whole difficulty, not disturbing a single figurine or upsetting a single candy dish.

Who was the woman? She did not know, and she scolded herself for her foolish suspicions. Maybe the woman was a phantom of her own mind, a morbid suspicion that should be rooted out with prayer. Amos toying with some wanton temptress! It illbefitted a strong woman to entertain such terrible thoughts.

But now she began hunting the stray hair on his suits, closely examining his collars and cuffs. She even poked about in his pockets. And every time she did, shame and mortification engulfed her. She discovered nothing, and knew that her suspicions were but the chimeras of her fevered imagination. Why wouldn't her fears subside? They grew, week by week, until sometimes she spent whole evenings conjuring up this wraith, this shadowy creature who was stealing Amos from her.

Being a strong woman, she resolved to improve matters in a practical fashion. She wanted her wayward husband, first citizen of Archuleta County, to devote more time to her. Love no longer mattered. She wanted his companionship.

That summer, a particularly balmy one in Paradise, she realized that if she really wanted to hold on to her marriage, it would be up to her to rebuild it. And if she failed . . . well, she would put off thinking about that.

She resolved to begin during their regular Sunday dinner, the one time of the week she knew he would be present. They customarily attended the First Presbyterian Church in the morning, occupying exactly the same pew three rows back and directly in front of the pulpit, and then spent that day together, sometimes playing checkers.

The minister, Mr. Howard, had preached a fine sermon that July Sunday on the healing miracles in the Bible. She wished God would decide to heal her arthritis, but Mr. Howard had an answer for that: if we weren't healed of a physical problem, it was because God wanted to use it to help us grow. Hadn't he refused to heal Saint Paul? She was tired of the pain. She wanted relief.

Mrs. Cutler, their domestic, served up chicken and dumplings, and when Amos had polished those off, Myrtle began her campaign.

"I should like to see your new office suite, Amos," she said.

"Oh, it's just a business place with a few extra amenities."

"Well, I intend to see it anyway. I want to know where my husband spends so much of his time, day and night."

He smiled affably. "Very well. Tomorrow at noon,

when I have no engagements, come have a look. I hope you'll admire my decorating."

"It must be a burden to clean, Amos. I'll send Mrs. Cutler to go over it once a week."

"Oh, I've taken care of that, my dear. Don't worry your pretty head about it."

"Do the bank janitors do it?"

"No."

"Well, I'll come tomorrow and add a woman's touch. I think I'll come more often."

"Oh, that's a kind thought, Myrtle, but quite impossible. I am presently transacting half a dozen deals, some of them very sensitive. You can't just barge in—"

"I'll knock," she said. "You could spend more time at home with me, you know. I'm feeling rather left out."

"I'll make an effort to do so."

She smiled. "I'm sorry it's an effort," she said. "I wish you might just find refuge from the world in my company."

"I do, Myrtle."

"I tell you what—you entertain your business partners here, and I'll have Mrs. Cutler serve spirits whenever you ring the bell."

"Ah, that won't—"

"Amos. I insist. We've drifted much too far apart. I'm alone and people are noticing."

"They are, are they?"

"Yes, scarcely a day goes by without someone or

other asking after you or sympathizing with me. It's causing some gossip."

"It does? Why should anyone care?"

She smiled at him. He knew perfectly well why. The most prominent citizen in Paradise did not live unobserved.

"I should like to take a trip, Amos. You've money enough."

"Well, nothing's stopping you."

"I do not wish to travel alone. What joy is there in that?"

He toyed with his dumpling. "I don't have the time for it."

"You don't have time for me? After putting Mr. Knott in your seat precisely to give yourself more time?"

"Maybe we could take a little train trip to Ouray."

"I'd like a trip to Europe. We could visit Dilworth in England. Poor boy. We've neglected him. We could take a Cunard steamer across the sea, or a White Star, and watch the waves and the porpoises and sit in deck chairs. We could see London, maybe see Victoria. Imagine seeing a queen! And take a trip across the channel and see the French. I hope they're clean."

"But I truly can't leave here, Myrtle."

"I take it that Mr. Knott is not doing well, then, and must be watched."

"Well, he's rather new to the task."

"Why'd you pick him? You'd scarcely mentioned him before, and then suddenly, you made him cashier and vice president and turned over the reins. I thought surely you'd pick someone with more executive experience, like Lucullus Partridge, or Wolf Dawes. Why on earth did you do that?"

"Don't worry your pretty head about it, Myrtle. I spend time here each Sunday to escape the cares of the world. So we mustn't talk of those things."

"It's very odd. Suddenly your teller is running the bank. You must esteem him highly."

"He's a good man. You should invite his wife into your circles. But all that is business, and I don't wish to bore you with these dreary things. You leave all that to me. I do my best to keep you in peace and safety and contentment. Is there any luxury you lack, including indoor plumbing?"

"Yes, I lack you. I'm going to expect you at home from now on. For one thing, I want to stop people from thinking things they shouldn't. For another, I miss your company, and you miss the ordinary pleasures of a comfortable home, which I have proudly given you."

He poked at his food. "Maybe I can spend an evening now and then. We can play cribbage. You'll whip me regularly, I'm sure."

"No, Amos, not just now and then. If you care for me, then spend time with me. Make *me* your business!"

She went farther than she had intended with that sally, and it hung there nakedly. But she didn't retreat. Her marriage was imperiled. He was cruelly neglecting her. It was time for him to know it.

He gave her that affable smile intended to wash away objections and reached across the table to touch her. "You're my own Myrtle," he said, "and always will be."

She smiled back. "We'll see," she said.

Chapter 6

Eloise Joiner had grown up in a hurry. You had to mature fast when you lived on the edge of an abyss. Until she married she had never had a home and had never lived in a town she could call her own. She had never had a moment's security or comfort, and rarely had she eaten a proper meal.

From the earliest age, all she had possessed was her one skimpy dress. She had dreamed of a wool coat and shoes and mittens and a felt hat, always knowing she could not have them. She had never known a family hearth or kitchen. She had lived in tawdry rooms, alcoves, shacks, barns, chicken coops, haylofts, basement storerooms, factory sheds, sidetracked cabooses, and sometimes under the stars because her father, Algernon Battle, had found no other place for them to stay.

Battle was a widower, Eloise his sole child. His wife had died of despair and rested in a potter's field in Atchison, Kansas. Eloise had never seen her mother's unmarked grave.

Algernon Battle was simply the laziest man on earth. He could not bring himself to labor for a living. Humble work was not for him. He survived with the gift of gab. Most everyone liked him—at first. He could charm ladies, wallop out a good joke, spin tales that enchanted his listeners. He was a born raconteur, and he used his gifts as a substitute for labor. They won him an occasional bowl of grub or a sour beer in a saloon.

If these skills failed him, he fell back on promises. He would promise a hostler to shovel out a stall, promise a cord of firewood to a housewife, promise to help load a boxcar, promise to mop an office or swamp a saloon. These promises were the coin that got him a place to stay for a while, meals for his daughter now and then, cast-off clothing, and whiskey when he was parched. But he rarely kept his promises.

Eloise grew up alone, living in a fantasy world full of skirts and blankets and scrambled eggs and milk. At an early age she saw through her father. By the age of nine, she had traded her own labor for food. She discovered that hoeing or weeding a garden was worth a good hot meal, and running an errand could win her a nickel. Once or twice an older woman took her in when her father had vanished, but these joyous interludes never lasted long. By the age of eleven she had discovered that men had designs on girls. By the age of thirteen she was on her own.

There had been a miracle in all this: in the midst of the squalor, Eloise was transforming herself into a lady. She understood the world better than most women of any age ever did. She knew the value of work, of honor, of courage, and of integrity. These qualities were the coin that paid off in comfort and happiness. So she waitressed, sewed, clerked, cooked, husked corn, scrubbed floors, kept accounts, and fed hogs, and whenever an employer cheated, or some galoot laid an unwelcome hand on her, she headed for the next job, gaining courage and confidence all the while. She never saw her father again.

She had drifted west, and near Hays, Kansas, had met a young bachelor rancher named Rolf Joiner, who hired her to cook and clean for his three-man bachelor crew. She had told him bluntly that if any one of them made an improper advance, she would not only leave immediately, she would report it.

They respected that. Later, Rolf told her she was the toughest young lady he had ever come across. Rolf Joiner provided a cottage and a twenty-a-month wage plus board. But he provided more. Joiner had a rakish humor, a gift for singing, merry blue eyes, coppery hair, and a way with women.

She married him gladly.

The world had finally become a friendly place.

The flat prairies around Hays eventually bored them, and they headed west, driving Rolf's herd of

Shorthorns before them. The westering instinct was strong in them, and in everyone they knew. Head west, into the sunset, and life would be better. They ranched a while near La Veta, Colorado, and then headed west yet again, looking for better pasture. They found it in 1879 in Archuleta County. The verdant valley caught their eye, and the creeks rushing out of the San Juan Mountains promised water year-round. They bought a place that had just been proven up and got a mortgage from the Merchant Bank of Paradise to pay for it. There they ranched, gradually fenced their pastures, admired the mountains, danced the fiddlers' tunes with their neighbors, and prospered.

And then Rolf died of a massive stroke in 1886.

Eloise grieved and vowed to carry on. There were a dozen men within half a dozen miles who would have married her on the spot. But she had never forgotten the lessons of her miserable childhood. For one reason or another, none of the local bachelors measured up, and in any case she grieved for Rolf and didn't feel like marrying again. With Rolf she had her freedom and her responsibilities, and she was not about to give up a bit of what she had won at such a cost.

But ranching required labor, sometimes strong male labor when the branding and castrating had to be done. She found that the things that Rolf had done so effortlessly, other men did poorly. Calves died under the knife or the hot iron. Some of her stock vanished. She was forever rebuilding her fences and chasing other beef off her land.

When the Jaekels approached her, wanting to lease her pasture, she thought she saw a way out. Sell her stock and rely on the rent. But for once she had been naïve. The Jaekels brutally overgrazed her land, underpaid her, using a thousand petty arguments to whittle down their payments, and then reduced their rentals, saying the sagebrush-choked pasture was worthless. Eloise fell behind on her mortgage. Several fiery confrontations with the Jaekels yielded nothing; she was unable even to evict them, but too independent to seek help.

That was when Amos C. Burch drove up to her decaying ranch house, once the apple of her eye, and hat in hand, told her in a soft and sorrowful voice that he was forced to foreclose and evict. In a flash, the year of desperate and lonely struggle, one woman wrestling with an entire herd and rapacious neighbors, all came to naught.

She had hung on to the back of her morris chair, fearful that she would collapse, terrified that she would have to return to the desperate life of her girlhood.

"Very well," she said softly. "Tell me when I must leave, and what I may keep."

"The mortgage covers only the land and buildings, not your personal effects. You have furniture, a spring wagon, two draft animals . . ."

"Thank you, Mr. Burch. And how much time have I?"

"Well, I'm forced to foreclose today—we have no choice as we must protect our depositors' funds. I feel so saddened by this. How hard it is for you. Believe me, I'd do anything I could to avoid this. Life's painful. You need not be in a hurry to leave. And if you need a large dray, I'll send someone out and have your things brought to town. I can't tell you how this tortures me."

He was sincere. She knew that. Amos Burch's excellent reputation did not rest on sand. It had been formed out of scores of acts of kindness and generosity, unceasing rectitude, temperance, and a devotion to the well-being of Paradise and the whole county.

"I have a headache," she said. "Send the dray on Saturday."

She could never quite explain to herself what happened then. She was in tears, hugging him fiercely, and he was holding her tight and comforting her. And then came blistering heat. When, a moment later, they pulled apart and stared into each other's eyes, the entire world became new.

In one miraculous afternoon, she recovered her ranch, acquired a new and reliable tenant, got rid of the Jaekels, and enjoyed a strong lover and protector. It made her dizzy.

She did not love Amos Burch, but she discovered in him a friend and mate. She was flattered by his attention and his passion. He filled an aching void in her, one she had fought and denied and hidden from herself. But after those first high-summer days of columbines and roses, the real world filtered in.

Suddenly she had a secret. Suddenly everything she did was calculated to conceal. Suddenly she was the other woman, not a wife—the kind of woman the world called *fallen*. Her occasional furtive trips to Paradise, where she and Amos raptured in his upstairs double-locked suite, reminded her that she could never dine with him at the Log Cabin Restaurant; never hail him on Cedar Street; never go to town without some flighty excuse, such as shopping; never settle beside him at meetings, church services, christenings, funerals, rallies, dances, lectures. Not ever. Had she made a devil's bargain? It had all happened so suddenly, in a moment of vulnerability.

And yet . . . he cared. He nurtured her, brought bonnets and crinoline and lace, protected her against a sea of troubles. That was enough for the moment, but not for the long term. She was still young, life stretched ahead to fine sweet horizons. But what good was all this?

"Amos," she said one evening when she had slipped into town, "we must think of the future. Of you and me, with no secrets hidden from Paradise. This can't last, you know."

He lay beside her, breathing peacefully. His broken nose, so incongruous with his other parts and his reputation, always fascinated her. She ran a finger over it.

"Can't last?" he asked.

"It's not right for either of us. I can't live out my life as a veiled woman all alone at Thanksgiving and Christmas. I'd like a husband, a home, and no secrets at all. Not one. If you love me . . ."

"That's not possible, Eloise. Divorce is unthinkable for me. It'd be a scandal. Not one soul would approve of it. Myrtle is my treasure, you know. It's true things have, well, slipped, but she suffers the arthritis and can't be, ah, what you are to me.

"You've given me more joy than I've known in years. You make me young again. You make me whistle tunes. In time, you'll see how good this is for us both. I am very happy. I ask nothing of you except to be mine, Valentine."

"Amos," she said, "you're asking more than I can give."

He held his peace and responded with a squeeze of his hand. "Let me steer our course," he said. "It will be safe and sure."

"No, we've already been seen."

He laughed softly. "Daniel Knott will never be a problem."

She said nothing. To her way of thinking, a secret was no longer a secret when anyone—anyone at all—knew of it. It would only be a matter of time. If Daniel Knott knew, then his wife knew, and if she knew, the world would know.

She didn't particularly like this suite, which exuded an aroma of cigars, spittoons, and greenbacks. It had been luxuriously decorated with flocked wallpaper, oak wainscoting, thickly padded leather furniture, and this marital-size four-poster in a small rear room that seemed to swallow the feeble yellow light of the coal-oil lamp. The place trapped secrets, and now it trapped hers.

"Amos," she said, "I would like you to make an honest woman of me." She said it lightly but firmly.

"Dear Eloise . . . give me time," he replied.

She suspected there would not be much time to give.

Chapter 7

Something insidious was happening to her marriage, but Hannah Knott could not put a name to it. It had all started with that sudden promotion and raise. At first, everything seemed grand. Money flowed into the family coffers. She didn't hesitate to buy shoes for her children or treat them to the J. A. Bailey Three Ring Circus when it stopped for a matinee and evening show in Paradise. She had never before known luxury, and now it wrought smiles in her.

And yet something had changed. Daniel had folded into himself, and intimacy had vanished from their union. Up until that promotion they had shared everything. He had his daily war stories to tell: Mr. Burch's little kindnesses, and sometimes peccadilloes. The customer who couldn't balance his accounts. The woman who saved pennies for years and then bought a straw hat with her savings.

The time some desperadoes entered, terrified everyone, and then fled when they saw Mr. Parkins, the constable, down the street.

But now Daniel had turned taciturn and even dour. Through the long, glaring summer in Paradise, her husband had steadily withdrawn into his own world, as if he possessed secrets he could not share and bore burdens too heavy for his shoulders.

Several times she had tried to confront him, but he had swiftly deflected her questions. Now they lived apart, sharing the same house but not the same marriage. She grew desperate, wanting her Daniel back. The future looked hollow, even though she found herself being welcomed into stately homes she had never set foot in before, by women who now numbered her among their own.

One glowing August Sunday, when the children were off to the mountains on a church picnic and she and Daniel were alone in the house, she tried a new tack.

"Daniel, I'm going to visit my parents while I still can. They're not getting any younger."

"That's a long trip," he said.

"We can afford it. I intend to stay there."

"You'll come back in a few weeks, when school starts again, of course."

"Maybe not. I may take the children with me. I am not happy here. We need some time apart."

Daniel was shocked. "But why? You have everything now."

"You know why."

She was brimming with tears and anger but fought back her feelings.

He pulled her to the sofa and tried to comfort her, but she sat rigid and erect and refused to let him put his arms around her, though she was famished for his embrace.

"If I've failed you, I'm sorry."

"Oh, Daniel, you have no idea what it's like to be kept out of your life. We used to share everything. There were no secrets between us."

He sighed, saying nothing.

"Ever since you got that promotion you haven't had one happy day. You're affecting the children. They want to know what's wrong, why doesn't Daddy like them anymore? They're doing poorly in school. Peter's become unruly. I can't handle this alone, Daniel. They'll be better off with their grandparents."

Stricken, he stood suddenly, pacing round and round the new Brussels carpet, strangely agitated and upset. She watched, bewildered, unable to fathom what terrible termite was eating away his heart and soul, gnawing at their marriage, shutting her out of his life.

Then, suddenly, he stopped. He seemed to wilt as he returned to the sofa, as if his courage had fled him.

"I didn't realize . . ." he began.

She kept her silence. He obviously was struggling with something terrible.

He ran a hand through his disheveled hair.

"There are several men more qualified than I to run a bank. I think I was promoted for darker and more cynical reasons. The raise and promotion were probably intended to buy my silence, by making my situation so attractive that I wouldn't dream of jeopardizing it. And it's tearing me to bits."

At last, something, some small clue. She had waited since June for this, even as the Knott family fell to pieces.

He sat silent for so long that she wondered if he would ever open up. Then he buried his face in his hands and sagged.

"Mr. Burch . . . isn't the man . . . I had always looked up to," he said. He peered about wildly, as if to check for eavesdroppers. But they were alone in the cool parlor on a hushed Sunday afternoon, breezes wafting through the open windows, with the benevolence of Paradise swaddling them like an infant's blanket.

"You see—" he said, halting, to lift his hands helplessly, and then he finally began droning the story. About Mr. Burch's payment of the Joiner mortgage to stave off foreclosure. About his afternoon trips in his black buggy, and his increasing absences. And then about what had occurred near the end of June.

Daniel described what happened in harsh, uncompromising terms.

It had shocked Daniel, but the revelation didn't shock Hannah at all. She had long ago concluded that behind Amos Burch's facade lay much more than a benevolent soul, that there was an iron fist encased in his velvet glove as well as appetites nurtured by unbounded wealth and power. But Daniel had obviously been shocked to the bone, disappointed, disillusioned. His idol had clay feet.

Poor Mrs. Joiner. Did she have the faintest idea what all this would lead to? Hannah pitied her. Whispering could drive a woman to an early grave.

Daniel plunged in again, his voice harsh and unyielding. "I wondered and worried all the next day what might happen. I feared that I might be discharged. But that didn't happen, Hannah. Instead, he asked me into his office and blandly promoted me. Not just a little raise, but right to the top. Oh, he never said a word about what I had seen. All he talked about was my ability. But I knew well what all this was about. He gave me a day to think it over. I came home that night half crazy. If I turned him down, he would discharge me and there would be questions in your eyes, and maybe some very hard times for us. And if I accepted . . ."

"Oh, Daniel."

He looked at her bleakly. "Now you know."

"Daniel, all that matters to me is that we're together again. Don't ever keep a secret like that from me again! Whatever you do, I'll be with you. We'll make our life together. Just don't wall yourself off from me, that's all I ask."

She wiped tears from her eyes as he pulled her hand into his. "I think I've done something wrong," he said. "Nothing was ever said. I made no promise to Amos, but there was . . . an unspoken transaction. I keep asking myself whether I did something wrong."

"You were only thinking of us, Amos."

"Yes," he said, and she sensed such desolation in that one word that it shocked her. "I was trapped. If I didn't accept that promotion, I'd be fired. He said so. Accept or leave! I have you and the children to support. And I told myself I never agreed to anything."

"What do you want to do?" she asked.

"Leave."

"Right away?"

He shook his head. "I need to prove myself here as a bank manager first. But in a year or so, we'll move away. This secret is a millstone around my neck. Every day I go to work knowing something about my employer I wish I didn't know. Knowing that the man who is idolized by the whole town has a weakness. That he expects me to hide it, and remain absolutely loyal. I . . . I know I can do the job, even if that isn't why I was promoted. I just want to prove it. And then go. Leave this place, this Eden."

"Yes, it's an Eden, and Mr. Burch has made it so," she said. "But he's also the serpent. Dan, we shouldn't think of this place as the Garden of Eden. Adam and Eve were innocents, and when they stopped being innocents, God turned them out and they couldn't return, and the gate to Eden was guarded against them. I'm afraid of what's going to happen when the people of Paradise find it's not paradise. We'll have to name the town Gossip, Colorado!"

He smiled for the first time in a long while. This quiet afternoon of communion had lifted a burden from him.

"I guess I'll put off the trip," she said.

That sealed everything. She sighed as something clawing at her soul released itself.

"Hannah? If we save all we can, in a year we'll have enough to get along while I find a new position. Then we can move."

"We'll save. We don't need anything, anyway."

Another week slid by, and then she found herself taking tea with Myrtle Burch, who had sent her card bearing an invitation.

Myrtle Burch's appearance shocked her. The woman had borne her arthritis with such cheer for so long that Hannah had admired her. But now she looked gray, with ashen pouches under her eyes. But the smile was unfeigned.

"How is Mr. Knott doing?" Myrtle asked, as Mrs. Cutler poured tea.

"Well, it's a burden, but he's managing."

"It was such a surprise. Amos never said a word. Never hinted. But you know how men are."

"It surprised Daniel just as much. He really had no idea—"

"Well, he certainly impressed my husband. You're married to a very gifted man, Hannah."

Hannah smiled. The Earl Grey tea soothed her. Sitting in this sun-dappled parlor, decorated with elegant taste, pleased her. But she sensed that all this was leading somewhere.

"Did Mr. Knott ever say why he was elevated so suddenly?"

Hannah's pulse raced. "Yes," she said.

Myrtle Burch waited and sipped and smiled expectantly. But Hannah let the moment pass.

"It was all so sudden," Myrtle said. "Impulsive. So unlike Amos."

"Mr. Burch has other things on his mind than banking," Hannah said.

"I wish I knew what," said the wife of the man who employed Hannah's husband.

Maybe if you knew, you would wish you didn't know, Hannah thought.

Chapter 8

From all outward appearances, Myrtle Burch's life flowed placidly onward. The first lady of Paradise reigned over the distaff side of her town as if born to the task. To this rude frontier settlement in Colorado she brought graces distilled from her childhood in Hartford, Connecticut. She had grown up in the shadow of the old statehouse, designed by Charles Bulfinch. The daughter of an insurance man who died young, she had met Amos in Hartford when they were both practically children. He had worked for Samuel Colt in some ill-paid junior executive capacity, and dreamed of the Golden West. All those revolvers were heading west, into a wild land, and Burch's heart went with them. That was how, ultimately, they arrived in Archuleta County, Colorado, where the whole world was young and virginal.

She pined for Hartford but never said a word. If

only she could return to an old city thick with friends and loved ones, sisters and brothers, nieces and nephews, she might yet find bliss. But she didn't know how to flee Paradise or free herself from the clutches of a man who had discarded her for a woman whose name she did not know.

Divorce would be a most difficult undertaking. What could be the grounds? She could not fault Amos for desertion or cruelty or abandonment. Nor was he mad or a felon. He didn't have bad habits. Not even bad breath. Not Amos. All the usual reasons for separating were closed to her. What on earth would the pampered first lady of Paradise offer as grounds?

It wouldn't help any that Burch's penny-ante poker crony Prescott Boardman would preside. She knew Judge Boardman would laugh her suit out of court. Nor would it help matters that Boardman sat on the boards of several of Amos's companies, including the waterworks. Nor would it help that Amos employed two of the three lawyers practicing in that county seat.

So she did what a resourceful woman of means could do: little by little, she probed into Amos's private life. The vague sense that he was dallying with someone would not go away, though she was as far from any real evidence as ever. She dreaded a scandal, and half hoped her intuitions were untrue. A straying husband could well be an indictment of a wife. But if adultery were the only charge she could bring against him that would win her a

new life, she would do it, resolutely and coura-
geously. She was not a weak-willed woman.

So she probed. One Saturday evening at a Knights
of Pythias potluck supper, she corralled Alden
Streeter.

"How is the new man at the bank working out?"
she asked.

The balding, portly barrister puzzled that a moment. "Why, I don't really know. That was a surprise, wasn't it?"

She sensed that he was fishing.

"Yes, indeed. Amos had barely mentioned
Daniel Knott to me. Did he discuss the promotion
with the directors?"

"Not a word, Myrtle. I couldn't imagine what
got into Amos's head. Of course he keeps a close
eye on things. I suppose he saw merit in the young
man."

"But it was so sudden. And just one big leap.
One day Daniel Knott was a teller and bookkeeper,
next day he was vice president and cashier and
running the bank."

"Well, who knows, Myrtle? Amos isn't one to reveal his cards. And who are we to ask? If it weren't
for Amos Burch, this county would still be raw
wilderness."

"Ask him sometime, Alden. Wives are always
the last to know anything."

There was a certain ironic tone in her voice that,
she knew, sailed past the attorney.

"I might just do that," Streeter said. "Actually, I

like the young fellow. And his wife—a real charmer. I think Amos simply has a good eye for ability."

"He has a good eye, all right," she said, a small, twisted smile building on her lips.

So she had learned something: Amos's elevation of Knott had been precipitous and private. She gleaned little more from Hannah Knott, who seemed reluctant to talk about Daniel's position, almost as though she were afraid that Myrtle might learn too much. Hannah Knott knew something she was unwilling to share.

Twice during their little talks, Myrtle had caught Hannah staring at her with something on her face that looked like pity. *Pity!*

Myrtle took to strolling during those late-summer evenings, defying her arthritis. She made sure that her tours always took her along Cedar Street past the Merchant Bank of Paradise, and past the separate door that opened onto the stairwell to the upstairs. These tours yielded nothing. She discovered no dray or wagon or horse parked close to the bank. She rarely saw a lamp lit in the second-floor windows. Where was Amos and what was he doing? He was not burning the midnight oil as he claimed, she told herself.

One day she wandered into the bank and asked the purse-mouthed teller, Jasper Pickering, whether she might see Amos's accounts. She thought there might be an error, she explained.

The young fellow smiled unctuously. He had

rarely conversed with Paradise's leading lady. "Why, certainly, Mrs. Burch."

The teller hastened away to get the proper ledger, while Myrtle waited nervously, hoping Daniel Knott wouldn't show up. Pickering returned with the ledger and seated Mrs. Burch at a worktable behind the teller wickets, where she could peruse the Burch accounts at her leisure. Everything seemed in order, at least to her unpracticed eye. She discovered no large transfer of funds at the time in June when Daniel Knott had suddenly been promoted.

She was about to surrender when she remembered something that had been as floating and ephemeral in her mind as cottonwood cotton. That spring, Amos had yet again showed great kindness and rescued a widow in distress from foreclosure. She sometimes teased Amos about all his benevolences, and he always nodded, amused, and said little. Word of the deed had eventually filtered through Paradise.

Yes, there it was: six hundred dollars transferred to one Eloise Joiner, some weeks before Knott had suddenly become the manager of the bank. She had met Mr. and Mrs. Joiner several times. An attractive couple, with one grown son who'd left the area. Mrs. Joiner radiated something better understood by men than by women. Eloise Joiner . . .

And that was when she looked up and discovered Daniel Knott staring at her.

"Oh, Mr. Knott. I'm just wondering about our accounts."

He peered over her shoulder upon the April entries.

"That's rather far back, isn't it?"

"I just was wondering whether there was an error. I suppose not," she said.

He looked uncomfortable. "We keep perfect books, Mrs. Burch. Is there anything specific that you want to know?"

"It seems Amos is a very charitable man. I had no idea he gave so much away."

"That is not for me to say, ma'am. You may wish to talk to him directly. We, of course, can't be showing our accounts to people."

She smiled. "Not even to Amos's wife?"

"Well, no, actually. Not unless the account's in your name." He seemed on edge.

"Here," she said. "I'm done. I found what I wanted."

"And what was that?"

"Amos's gift to Mrs. Joiner."

Knott seemed to freeze. Then he swiftly plucked up the ledger.

"I have a very generous husband, it seems. But he never tells me much about his charity."

Knott nodded.

"Mr. Knott—you look like a man who wants to say something."

"Oh, well, ah, Mr. Burch has given so much to Paradise. I think I know of fifty little gifts. And some big ones. Of course, I can't talk about these things, except to you."

"Yet Amos doesn't tell me about them," she said dryly.

"Well, ah, I'm glad we could be of service. I'll tell Mr. Burch—"

"No. Say not a word. I just am interested in learning about our . . . shall I call them little charities? I'm always the last person in Paradise to learn about them, so I think I'll take matters into my own hands now. I've been insisting that we visit England, but Amos won't budge. You know what he said? How about a trip to Ouray? I think he gives too much away."

Knott looked ready to fall to pieces, and she let up. "You've been most helpful. If ever you wish to drop by and advise me about things—accounts, what's happening at the bank, troubles—please do. I hear so little of it from Mr. Burch."

"Oh, I wouldn't have anything to say."

Daniel stood there, nervous and fretting, and she knew she had pushed the man one notch too far, as usual. First ladies of small towns can always get away with things.

"Are you enjoying your promotion, Mr. Knott?"

"Yes, yes, I'm so grateful—"

"It was such a surprise. Mr. Burch must have been grooming you for years, preparing you for the big moment."

"Ah, no, ma'am. It was quite a surprise."

"Really? Then he must be very confident in you."

"I, ah, I really must get back to work. Call on me anytime."

"Where did you learn how to make safe loans and collateralize them, Mr. Knott?"

He looked relieved. "Actually, Mr. Burch is teaching me."

"I see. He treats you like a son."

"Oh, I wouldn't say that, Mrs. Burch. He's just one kindly employer, that's all."

"There must have been something else." She smiled as he startled. Daniel Knott was the most ill-at-ease man she had encountered in months.

"Mr. Knott, I would like to invite you to drop by for tea anytime. If there's ever something you wish to whisper about, we'll just have a little tête-à-tête. I'm always interested in the bank. And I love secrets."

"Yes, surely, Mrs. Burch."

She took her sweet time leaving while Daniel hovered about, ill at ease. She plucked up her white parasol, headed for the big double doors, and waved cheerfully at the nervous new vice president of the bank.

She knew he knew something. He could unravel the mysteries she was encountering, if only he would. He was the key to her divorce if what she suspected was true: that Daniel Knott had caught Amos in the middle of an adulterous affair. Either Knott was blackmailing Amos—which she doubted—or

Amos had swiftly elevated him as a way of buying his silence. Adultery was a good ground, and maybe in Daniel she had a *witness*.

But for now she had no proof. And nothing with which to win her freedom.

Chapter 9

Myrtle Burch took her marital vows seriously, and when the mood struck her, she pushed aside the thought of divorce whenever it rose, unbidden, in her mind. What did she lack? Nothing. She could be the contented wife, first lady of Paradise, for all the rest of her years.

But her heart ached so much that she scarcely even thought of the constant pangs of her arthritic body. Slowly, resolve crystallized within her soul: no matter what the scandal, no matter what the shock to Paradise, she would end this charade of a marriage. The town would never be the same, but maybe that was a good thing. Adam and Eve did not live for long in Eden, after all, and no other mortals should either.

She scarcely knew where to turn. Surely not Alden Streeter or Mark St. John, both of them family friends and the very attorneys Amos entrusted with his considerable business. On more occasions than she could remember, she had entertained Alden and Bess Streeter, and Mark and Ambrosia St. John, spending affable evenings playing whist or pinochle.

That left only Eben Lytell, the third of Paradise's three lawyers; a young, brusque Lincolnesque outsider who had moved to the county two years earlier, finding clients among the less favored of the town's residents. Lytell it would be. The others would politely decline and run to Amos the moment she had left their offices. She supposed Lytell would, too. But the man had handled a few small torts against Burch businesses, and that was a good sign.

She waited yet another day, testing her feelings, fearful of the unknown, well aware of what power Amos possessed. She had some funds in the Merchant Bank, piggy-bank money she had set aside just for herself. She withdrew the considerable sum of three hundred dollars, in the form of double eagles. The young teller, Pickering, didn't ask any questions.

She then arrived unannounced at Eben Lytell's home on San Juan Avenue. He practiced law from the parlor of his home, perhaps to save a bit on rent. Or perhaps to avoid being beholden to Amos, who owned most of the business property in Paradise.

He appeared swiftly in shirtsleeves and a black waistcoat, lean, raffish, and vaguely troubled. She had never known him to be at ease socially.

"Mrs. Burch. So early in the morning. Please come in."

She penetrated a make-do office furnished with a well-worn desk and leather-backed swivel chairs, battered lawbook cases, and some old lithographs of locomotives.

"What may I do for you, Mrs. Burch? A donation, I imagine? So many worthy causes."

"A divorce."

He stopped cold, staring at her from the depths of his dark eyes, as if the candles in his noggin had been extinguished.

When he finally spoke, every word was measured, considered, cut, dried, skinned, and weighed before he uttered it.

"I'm not sure I'm the right attorney for you, Mrs. Burch."

"You're the only one in the county. The rest—" She smiled and he nodded.

"Your best move might be to find an attorney in Durango. Have him move the case to La Plata County. I'm sure you understand why."

"If you'll take the case and file here, I'll take my chances with Judge Boardman. In fact, La Plata County would be exactly where Amos would prefer to deal with it. Or even farther away."

Lytell puckered and unpuckered, putting the burden on her to continue.

"You're wondering what's wrong, what possible grounds I have. There aren't many, are there?"

He shook his head.

"I cannot sue for divorce on the basis of desertion, nonsupport, cruelty, madness, or conviction of a felony, now, can I? He doesn't smell like a barnyard, he washes faithfully, he doesn't beat me, he puts his used underdrawers in the hamper, and he brushes his incisors religiously. He doesn't belittle me in front of dinner guests. I will vouch for the inoffensiveness of his armpits. He even speaks to me now and then, slowly and carefully but without condescension. He has never treated me like a dog."

This time Lytell smiled, and the fires of curiosity boiled up in those slate-colored eyes. Still, he was finding it safer not to say a word.

"That leaves but one ground, Mr. Lytell."

"Do you have proof?"

"No, but I know who the woman is—I think I do, anyway—and I also believe there's a witness. Very mysterious. Whether the man will talk is anyone's guess. He is greatly beholden to Amos."

"Well, what do you know, and how do you know it?"

Swiftly she explained her difficulties, beginning with Amos's neglect; then his withdrawal from all intimacy; then his new life in the upstairs suite of the bank, complete with a four-poster and mosquito netting.

"That's not nearly enough," he said, sounding as though he wanted to close the conversation.

"There's more," she said. "Her name is Eloise Joiner."

"I know Mrs. Joiner. I did a little business for her."

"Does this present a conflict?"

"No. She just came to see whether she could evict some tenants. I advised her."

Slowly, deliberately, Myrtle made her case: Amos's sudden personal "charity" on the eve of foreclosure, followed by his frequent trips out on the Alamosa road, supposedly to check his properties. Then the sudden elevation of the teller, Daniel Knott, to a position of power, a move made without any consultation with the directors of the bank. A move so precipitous that it startled the whole town.

"Blackmail?" Lytell asked.

"I doubt it. Amos would tear a blackmailer to shreds and spit out the pieces. And anyway, Dan Knott's not the type. No, this was Amos's way of burying a secret so deep that it would never surface. I know from Mrs. Knott—Hannah—that her husband is under pressure. He's changed. He's hiding things from her. I sense he doesn't like his new post."

"A possible witness," Lytell mused. "Not much to go on, is it?"

"Could you ask him?"

"I could force him to testify under oath. But we can't just go fishing. Even if he saw something—we call it in flagrante delicto—we would still have a poor case. There's no corroboration. We could also get testimony from Mrs. Joiner. Maybe. There's a law against adultery, and she has the right not to testify against herself. Well, perhaps there's something to work with: your husband's swift and aberrational response to being found out. Are you sure there's nothing else?"

"No."

"And what do you want from this?"

"My freedom. I wish to return to Hartford. Some generous support. Lord knows he can afford it. And I want my good name to remain intact."

"Divorces are very muddy affairs, Mrs. Burch. Good names and reputations are the first to go to the scaffolds."

She swallowed back her fear. "I understand. I can pay you." She pulled out the purse with her double eagles.

He shrugged. "If Amos chooses to fight, your suit could cost much more."

"I have other personal property. Jewelry. A city lot."

Lytell stared out the window upon the utterly quiet residential avenue, and then swung back to face her. "Before I commit, I wish to think this over. I'm not at all sure I want this case. Win or lose, I might find myself forced to move my practice elsewhere, at great cost and difficulty. Amos Burch is one of the most powerful men in Colorado. Even worse things could happen."

"How long would it take you to decide?"

"Tomorrow."

"May I ask what your considerations will be?"

He shrugged. "My future in this county. If I bring your divorce suit, and we ground it on adultery, I am putting my head on the guillotine block." He grinned. "On the other hand, I did once aspire to be a lion tamer in a circus."

From that moment on, she adored him.

"I tell you what: I can decide this fairly swiftly. Your entire adultery case hinges on a witness. Do this for me, please. Bring Daniel Knott over, any-time, and we'll simply put it to him. What did he see? What was the reason for his sudden advance-ment? I am pretty good at reading a man who's squirming under my questions. Could you do that, Mrs. Burch? Then I'll know better whether to accept this, and whether I'm on solid ground."

She nodded. "I'll try, Mr. Lytell."

As they shook hands warmly, she discovered a small, sly grin in his chiseled face. It seemed he liked the odds after all.

Well, well, well, she thought as she strode toward the bank. She decided not to wait; if her case was to proceed, she would act at once.

She entered the wide doors, headed straight past the tellers' wickets, the safe, a rolltop desk, and down the short corridor to what had once been her husband's office. The heavy door was open, and she spotted Knott within, whittling a pencil.

"Mr. Knott, may I come in?"

"Mrs. Burch. Yes, of course. Good to see you." He bounded to his feet like an unloosed clock spring.

"I'm going to close the door, Mr. Knott. I have something private to discuss, and I am going to trust you with a secret."

He nodded uneasily.

"Mr. Knott, what I say here must not go anywhere else. May I count on you?"

He paused a long moment. "Yes," he finally said.

She wondered whether he meant it. She seated herself and waited for him to return to his swivel chair.

"There's no point in beating about the bush, Mr. Knott. I am going to bring a divorce action against my husband."

The new manager shrank visibly, but stayed calm. She could understand that: the town was about to face a scandal that would affect its business, politics, and even its social life forever.

"There is only one possible ground, Mr. Knott. Adultery."

She watched Daniel's lips clamp together.

"I believe you know something about that."

He stared, frozen.

"Do you, Mr. Knott?"

"Why do you ask, Mrs. Burch?"

"I've known about it for some while. My husband is involved with Eloise Joiner. I believe you are a man of merit, Mr. Knott, but I also believe your sudden promotion has something to do with what you know."

He seemed frozen, neither nodding nor shaking his head.

"I know certain things that you know, Mr. Knott. That Amos paid off Mrs. Joiner's mortgage and put her ranch on a profitable basis, for instance. The ledgers have told you that. I believe that his suite upstairs is used for . . . more than business.

"I believe your promotion was Amos's way of purchasing your silence and folding you into this town's elite. The only other interpretation is that you've blackmailed him."

"No! Good God, no!" he cried.

"Then come with me right now and talk to Eben Lytell."

Daniel sighed.

Chapter 10

Blackmail! Is that how Mrs. Burch and her lawyer were interpreting his rise to cashier? Daniel Knott intended to stop that sort of thinking in a hurry. Grimly, he accompanied Myrtle Burch the four blocks to Eben Lytell's office.

Blackmail? The very idea outraged him.

Lytell wasn't as well connected in Paradise as the other two attorneys. No wonder Mrs. Burch had selected him. She had no other choice. The attorney was a bachelor and was courting two young women at once.

Lytell swiftly ushered them into his parlor office, exuding good cheer.

"Mr. Knott, welcome. I gather Myrtle's told you that she's filing for divorce. The ground is adultery, and we believe you're the witness we need. Would you care to tell us about what you know and what you've seen?"

Knott boiled. "First of all, I want to stop this talk of blackmail. I was not given the promotion because of blackmail. In fact, I was reluctant to take the position at all, because I don't consider myself adequately seasoned. It was thrust on me."

"And for a reason, we believe."

Knott sagged. "I wish it weren't so. I would prefer to rise on my merits."

"Ah," said Lytell. "Now we're getting somewhere."

"That's as far as you'll get."

"Well, let's see, Mr. Knott. Amos Burch suddenly elevates you, gives you a remarkable salary, and puts you in command of a bank."

"He said only that he liked my work and wanted to spend more time on other things. That is *all* he said. No other matter was discussed. Nothing!"

"But there indeed was another matter."

Knott sighed. He would not lie. "Yes," he said.

"And was this matter connected in any way to Mrs. Joiner?"

"It's time for me to return to the bank, sir."

"We can compel your testimony in court, Mr. Knott."

Daniel tensed. His world was falling apart. He rued the day he had accepted the cursed promotion. "I will not discuss that. If I had not accepted the promotion, Mr. Burch would have discharged me on the spot. We have roots here. Hannah and I have neighbors and friends. This is our home."

"Why would Mr. Burch have discharged you?"

"He said he would. Accept it or leave, were his words."

"It was because you caught Mr. Burch and Mrs. Joiner in a compromising situation."

Knott refused to say anything, plainly regretted saying as much as he had already.

"Yes?"

Knott kept his silence.

"It looks more and more like blackmail to me, Knott, in spite of what you say."

"It wasn't!" Knott shouted.

"Then spare yourself some serious trouble."

"My conduct speaks for itself."

"I'm afraid it does. You witnessed something, and now suddenly you are the top man at the bank. What does that say?"

"There is such a thing as loyalty, sir. All my life I've been as loyal and faithful to my employer as I know how to be. I came here to tell you that blackmail never entered my mind, nor did I ever attempt it." He snapped it out with such force that both the attorney and Myrtle Burch fell into shocked silence.

"I've told you what I intend to tell you. I must return to my work now."

"I admire that, Mr. Knott. You know, Mrs. Burch would like your help. I'll speak confidentially to you now. She's had no marriage for years, if marriage means anything at all beyond sharing a house. She's soldiered along, raising her sons, but all the while she's been excluded from her husband's life, neglected in a thousand ways that have cut her deeply. But that's hard to prove by law. She hasn't taken this decision lightly, having kept her vows and endured through better and worse. All she wants is her freedom and some modest security after so many lonely years. But it turns out that isn't easy to accomplish. You see, there are no grounds for a divorce in this case—save one."

Knott nodded.

"We'll put our cards on the table for you, Mr. Knott. You stumbled onto the lovers in—shall we say, delicate circumstances—and I would guess this happened when you entered his office at some unusual hour. We have little doubt that he's involved with Mrs. Joiner. That sudden loan last spring, straightening out her affairs, and so forth. But it's all circumstantial. What we believe you saw is not circumstantial. You're an eyewitness. We're simply asking for your cooperation. We want it voluntarily and wholeheartedly. We can compel your testimony, and you'll be sworn and subject to perjury if you should fail to tell the whole truth. I can and will do that if necessary. But we would prefer your cooperation."

Knott scarcely knew how to answer.

Lytell waited patiently. Mrs. Burch sat primly, her lips pursed.

"Do you know what you are asking of me?" Knott said.

"A man of honor does what he must, no matter what the consequences."

"Do you know exactly what the consequences would be, Mr. Lytell?"

"Perhaps painful. But maybe Amos Burch will simply leave you alone. He is a good man, and he can weather a scandal well enough."

Myrtle stared out the window.

"I do not think he would permit me to continue at Merchant Bank. And I doubt that I could find other employment here. He owns so much of the business in this town and exerts so much influence on other merchants. So at the least, I would have to move elsewhere, disrupt my life and my family's life."

"A man of honor does what he must, Mr. Knott."

"I love my wife and children. They are secure and happy now."

"I know Amos as well as anyone," Myrtle said. "In most ways he is a splendid man. I don't think he would retaliate. In fact, he might privately esteem you for your moral courage."

Knott doubted it. His mind was awhirl. "Couldn't you build the case without me? There's plenty of evidence right in the bank ledgers."

"I wish we could," Lytell said. "But we can't. Your testimony is the very key to the divorce. It all rests on you."

"Why don't you dig up some new evidence? Surely someone could watch the rear entrance to the bank and report to you whenever he sees Mrs. Joiner and Mr. Burch enter. You could even talk to Mrs. Joiner, you know."

Lytell smiled. "Ah, to live in that sort of world,

Mr. Knott. She'll be named as corespondent, of course. I'm afraid you're the key."

"What options have I?" Knott asked.

"Just one. You can choose to live with your conscience, or defy it."

"I would to God that you offer me some way out. Not for my sake, but for Hannah's, for my children. For my good name."

"How could your name be tarnished?"

"People will think ill of me for testifying against Amos. I'll be considered ungrateful and malicious, especially after receiving such an opportunity from him."

Lytell grinned. He had an insouciant way about him that irritated Knott. "Well, Daniel—may I call you that?—you go think about it. We'd like a response tomorrow. I'm going to file the suit tomorrow, with or without your cooperation. And from that moment on, I can depose you."

Knott nodded. "And so can Mr. Burch's attorneys. I'm being ground between millstones."

"We deeply regret any pain you may feel."

"Oh, Mr. Knott, for my sake, please help us. I need your testimony so much. All my hopes, all my dreams . . ." Myrtle's voice trailed off.

"I will come here at noon with a decision," Daniel said.

He stormed back to the bank through a fine fall day, knowing already what he would do. The only question was how to tell Hannah that they would soon be leaving Paradise, probably dead broke, with his reputation in tatters.

He fretted through the rest of the day at the bank. As he hiked home after a wearying day, he wondered why the walk seemed uphill all the way.

That evening when they were alone in their bedroom, Daniel pulled Hannah to him and told her the whole story.

"Is there no way out?" she asked.

"I could lie, not once but over and over and over."

"That would kill you."

"Yes, it would. There's just something inside of me that tells me to do right. I have to live with myself, after all. I guess we may as well face the worst," he said.

"I'm scared, Daniel."

"Well, so am I. But let's live each day and each hour as best we can. We'll survive. And we'll keep our heads high."

She squeezed his hand. That was as good as a kiss, he thought.

The next morning he took a few minutes off from work and walked to Lytell's house. The matter was already resolved in his mind and he was at peace with his decision. He would stick to what he knew was true. He wasn't sure why he felt good about it. Maybe because that was how he had been trained. Maybe because he believed that a new land, like America, needed the kind of citizens who could make self-government work. Maybe it was religious conviction. He didn't know for sure.

He found Lytell busy with a client, and waited in the reception room, which was actually the foyer of his house. He was about to head back to the bank when Lytell's meeting came to an end. Moments later, Daniel Knott found himself staring into the eyes of the lawyer.

It took only two or three minutes to tell the simple story of his accidental discovery. There was no question about who the two were and what they were doing. Swiftly he outlined the next day's events, about the offer, and how Burch had cited Knott's skills as the reason for his promotion.

"Was there any quid pro quo?"

"None whatsoever, Mr. Lytell."

"But one was implied."

"Perhaps. But he never hinted at any reason other than a promotion based on merit."

"Did you tell your wife there might be another reason?"

"Yes, sir. We decided just to go along one day at a time. Mr. Burch is noted for his generosity and perhaps that was all there was to it."

"You will testify to all this?"

"Just as I've told you."

Lytell thrust out his hand. "I admire you, Knott. Good and honorable men are very few. Courageous men are even fewer. You had better expect trouble."

Chapter 11

The summons rocked Amos Burch. He could not believe his eyes. Myrtle was divorcing him! But why? And on what grounds? A chill ran through him. Surely she knew nothing.

Yet apparently she did. He studied the complaint and discovered the word he dreaded most: "adultery." It named Eloise Joiner as corespondent. How could Myrtle know? Shock, as black and ineradicable as India ink, washed over him, working outward from his heart into the arteries, veins, and capillaries, into the cells, seeping into his very flesh. He felt panic. Then seething rage. Betrayed by his own loins. Betrayed . . . by someone.

He could not let this proceed. The divorce would crack Paradise into pieces. He decided to have it out with Myrtle—a little forceful persuasion and she would drop the suit. If she insisted, a discreet separation, privately arranged, would suffice. No one would know.

He wondered whether it mattered if the world knew, and to ask the question was to answer it. He was an esteemed man, the county's first citizen, one of the leaders of Colorado, a man trusted and honored, a man begged to make commencement speeches, enticed to lead prayers and head committees. He might retain his business empire, but what would happen to his reputation?

He sank wearily into the swivel chair in his upstairs lair and tried to puzzle things through. The news would rocket around the courthouse like a roman candle, and it was too late to stop that. He wished he had paid more attention to Myrtle so that he could have headed this off.

Myrtle! Stealthily putting together her miserable little lawsuit while all the while supping at his table! He had only himself to blame. Too late to stop the gossip, but not too late to keep it out of the *Paradise Tattler*. He would talk to Plum, the editor.

Should he call Alden Streeter? He would have to, but this would take some measuring and cutting and tailoring. What he really wanted to do was twist Myrtle's arm a bit, get the thing withdrawn. Then he could halt the gossip in its tracks.

Amos Burch was rattled. In all the smooth years of progress in Paradise, this was the worst setback and the largest danger he had ever faced. He tried to quiet himself. He had that gift, which gave him the calmness he needed to triumph during crisis.

But how did she know?

No, he realized, that was the wrong question to ask. *Did* she know? Was this a guess on her part? Probably. She had not enjoyed his amorous attentions for some while, and had obviously grown suspicious. He spent his nights away from home, and that was enough to arouse the woman's ire.

But maybe she knew. Had he and Eloise been observed? It was quite possible, in spite of the extreme care they took. Rarely had Eloise even come to town. Most of their meetings had been out at her ranch, where they were all alone, miles from prying eyes.

And yet, he suspected Myrtle knew, somehow.

Now he would proceed with great care. He debated whether to call his attorney, and decided to wait, at least until he talked to his wife. Just to be sure of his footing, he studied the complaint again, then stuffed it into his breast pocket and strode through a lovely autumnal afternoon to his handsome home, which told the whole world exactly what Burch wanted to convey: that the squire of Paradise occupied that house. It was a Greek Revival home, with Doric columns and classic lines, a luxurious rarity in the frontier West.

He found her in the parlor, reading a romance.

"I've been expecting you, Amos."

"What is this?"

"I think you understand perfectly. I want my freedom and a good measure of security. I'm humiliated by your behavior, and I wish to return to Hartford."

"What behavior? Where did you get this non-sense?"

She stared mildly at him. "That will become apparent in court, Amos."

"I insist that you tell me."

"Talk to Mr. Lytell, Amos."

He began to pace the parlor, pausing before the Vermont marble fireplace, whirling past an oil portrait of his grandfather, sailing by the settee and the crewelwork rosewood chair.

"I refuse to let this proceed and I intend to stop it."

"Yes, you have Prescott Boardman in your pocket, don't you? Maybe you can call in all those favors you've done for the courthouse."

"Myrtle, let's settle this quietly, without stirring up Paradise. You'll be subject to the most vicious sort of gossip."

"Will I?"

"I'm afraid so. We both will. There's a simple solution. Just drop the suit and go visit in Hartford if that's what you want. Stay as long as you wish. I'll keep you funded. That's perfectly simple."

"But I want my freedom. You've broken the bond between us, not only with your Mrs. Joiner, but in a hundred other ways. What does she see in you, Amos? Money? You've deserted me."

"That's absurd."

"I will explain to the court just how I've been deserted."

He didn't like the way this was heading. "I want

you to call this off. If you persist, I'll fight it every inch of the way, with every dollar I possess."

"Yes, I expected that. You'll hide assets, tell Judge Boardman you're poor, and waste piles of money on counsel."

"And you'll soon be out of cash."

"Yes, that is true."

"Then it makes no sense, because I am damn well going to make sure this gets nowhere."

She seemed frightened for a moment, but then recovered her wits. "I am feeling a certain pleasure, Amos. At this point I would proceed just to see you squirm. You broke my heart cavorting with that woman, and now you'll see, as the saying goes, that 'hell hath no fury like a woman scorned.'"

"Did someone spread these lies about me?"

"No one has lied about you."

He didn't like that, either. The woman was showing an edge he had never suspected in her. "You have no case. But I'll tell you this: unless you drop this at once, you'll regret it for the rest of your life."

"Are you threatening me, Amos?"

He paused suddenly and sat down. "I'm sorry. You know, Myrtle, power is a corrupting force. I'm so used to having my way in this town that I think I can bully my way through troubles."

She seemed to soften a little.

"I'm thinking how good it would be to patch things up. I think of all the good years we've had, from the time we came here with little in our pockets, up until now, when this wild land is nearly settled and good American towns are rooting in good American soil. You're a pioneer, and so am I. We've built this land together, raised a family, and grown rich. But I've neglected you for business. What I'll do now is let the business run itself and spend my free hours with you."

"And what will you tell Mrs. Joiner?"

He sighed. He did feel remorse; it was not feigned. "Let us simply start over, Myrtle."

"It's too late. You abandoned your wife years ago, not just when you started visiting the Joiner ranch day after day, telling the world that you were up the valley looking at your properties."

"You seem to be guessing, Myrtle. You might be awfully wrong."

"I am not guessing."

"Then how do you know?"

"You've been seen."

Knott. It seemed unbelievable to him. Had Daniel Knott been blabbing to her? He would get to the bottom of this, and if it turned out to be Knott, then the man would find himself in worse trouble than he could ever have imagined. The ungrateful pup.

"Seen? Someone is either delusional or trying to extort something from you and me," he said. "Who was it?"

"Amos, we'll see you in court."

She spoke with such finality that he knew he could not badger a name out of her. Grudgingly, he admired her backbone.

He rose gently. "Let's put this right, Myrtle.

There's no need to drag our family through the mud. The boys will be mortified, and you'll wound me to the quick. Here's my offer. Go to Hartford. I'll send ten thousand dollars with you. Stay. If you wish, you may file for divorce after five years there in Connecticut, and I won't resist."

She stood, pain lancing her as she put weight on her knees. "No, Amos. I want my freedom now. We will proceed to a divorce trial."

He gathered his duster and hat and stalked away, leaving it for the maid to shut the door behind him. His mind was awhirl. Should he go to Streeter now, or confront Knott? He knew the answer even as he stormed back to the bank.

But his usual caution caught up with him as he walked. He didn't really know whether Daniel Knott had breathed a word to Myrtle or Lytell. Maybe there were other witnesses. He had better be careful. Threatening Daniel Knott might yield exactly the wrong result.

By the time he reached the bank late that October afternoon, his usual bland caution had triumphed. He subdued the turmoil within him. He would simply remind Knott of the many advantages he had as head of the Merchant Bank. He would phrase it in the gentlest manner, so carefully that no one could possibly say he was threatening a witness or obstructing justice. He had to be very careful. Not even Judge Boardman could save him from his own folly if he were reckless. Whatever he did, he must do alone. Neither Streeter nor Mark St. John could ever learn of his design.

Through the open door, he studied the young man a moment as Knott hunched over a letter he was writing.

"Well, Daniel, how are you doing?" he said.

Knott startled and turned to face Burch. For just a fleeting moment, Burch saw fear dance across the young man's face.

"All right, sir. I was just drafting a letter to Ephraim Noble. His mortgage payment's overdue."

"Very good. That's what I wanted to talk to you about. A man needs encouragement now and then. I've been gaining confidence in your work month after month. Right now, I would give you the highest recommendation I could draft. If ever Paradise seems too small for you, Daniel, count on me to assist you, just as you've assisted me all these months."

"Thank you, sir. I have no plans to move."

"Good. Then I can always count on you."

Knott just stared straight ahead.

Chapter 12

Daniel watched Hannah's face tighten as he told her about Burch's brief visit.

"The threat was so subtle that I almost missed it, but it was there. The price for telling the truth will be a swift discharge, without recommendation."

She nodded.

"The price for lying is perjury, which is a felony that could put me in prison, but for me it's much more. I have to live with myself. I've always tried to be an honorable man. I don't always succeed, but I try."

"We'll be poor?"

"Yes, unless I can find a position swiftly."

"Not here in Amos Burch's Paradise."

"No, not here, Hannah."

"I guess I'd better not spend a penny. It was so good to have some money in the bank. But you shouldn't worry about us. We'll get along somehow."

"Somehow? I don't know how, Hannah. A bad recommendation from a bank could follow me all my life. It's not like a bad recommendation from a drygoods store. Anyone in a bank, well, he has special responsibilities. Fiduciary trust. If Burch gives no reason for firing me, that makes it all the worse."

She reached out to touch him, and he felt her hand find his. He loved her dearly, and his children, and he ached to give them a good life. But now perhaps he never would be able to. He wondered whether he was being pigheaded or too full of pride, or too stuffed with ancient ideas about what makes a man a man.

"Hannah—I'm sorry. You and Peter and Rosalie and Daniel Junior will suffer. I can't help it."

"Daniel, I don't need much money, and we don't need status. We just need to hold our family together."

He headed toward the bedroom window. A cold wind blew outside, rattling the panes. Winter was coming. "Maybe nothing will happen," he said. "Maybe I read too much into a simple encounter with Amos. He's a good man. He's given so much to Paradise, helped so many people, kept the town free of undesirables."

"I don't think he's truly good," she said. "He has always had wealth and power and status. If those things are threatened, he'll stop at nothing."

"Oh, you just don't know him well," Daniel replied.

She didn't say anything, but he could tell she disagreed. She went back to combing her hair before the vanity mirror, stuffing the stray strands into her hair jar. She was trying to accumulate enough to have a fall made.

He stared at her, a lovely woman in her prim white cotton nightdress. He was about to bring thunderclouds into her peaceful life. And yet he had no choice. Or virtually none. He could resign and leave Colorado, settle beyond the writ of a Colorado court, and be safe. Burch had almost invited him to do it. Burch *wanted* him to do it. He could resign, leave, and once he crossed into New Mexico Territory he wouldn't have to appear under oath in a divorce trial. Wouldn't have to lie and face the murder of his own conscience or tell the exact truth and face the devastation that would swiftly be visited upon him.

"There is a safe harbor, Hannah."

She turned to him, her gaze searching his.

"I can resign and we can move out of the state before the trial. We would be safe."

"This is a very strange question, Daniel. If we did leave, would Myrtle Burch win her divorce?"

"I'm not a lawyer, so I can't say for sure. I don't think she would, without any clear evidence of Amos's trysts. But they might be getting more evidence somewhere."

An odd thing happened then. They stared at each

other, and they each knew he would stay and testify truly, all without a word being spoken. She smiled.

"I guess that was the right question," she said.

The Knotts would see that justice was done, no matter what the cost to themselves. Myrtle would be free to start her life anew. He considered it an odd decision. He scarcely knew Myrtle Burch. What possible good would come of it? Why was he throwing away his future for a suffering but distant woman?

He rummaged his mind for an answer, turning to civics, then to Thomas Jefferson's vision of the virtuous yeoman as the rootstock of a good republic. But in the end, those abstract ideas meant little. He would do what he had to do because it was right. He didn't even know where his notions of right and wrong came from, but he saw now that they certainly governed his conduct.

He would testify truthfully to what he had seen, and bear the consequences. He would simply tell the truth, and be the immovable rock.

He slept uneasily that night, vague alarms skittering through his mind about the safety of his children, the safety of Hannah, of his property, even of his own person. He had no reason to feel himself in physical jeopardy, and scolded himself for entertaining such nightmarish fantasies. But still they hovered there in the quiet darkness.

"Go to sleep," Hannah said.

But he couldn't.

During the next weeks nothing altered the placid

diurnal life of Paradise. The *Tattler* said not a word
about the impending divorce case. If gossip circu-
lated, it lay so buried that Knott never got wind of
it. Perhaps the city's business and courthouse elite
knew of the suit, but none of the rest of the town's
two thousand people knew anything. Amos Burch
continued to be the town's much-loved employer,
social leader, political gray eminence, and moral
exemplar.

Like so many towns in the bright new West, Paradise yearned for perfection. Wilderness made the
whole world new and fresh and as sweetly scented
as cedar. Paradise wasn't the cramped and settled
East: it was an alchemist's crucible, a place to burn
away bad institutions, overcome sin, fashion a
happy and safe community, and reach for the sublime. That had been Amos Burch's dream: heaven
on earth.

Daniel Knott had never quite subscribed to it.
Even in Paradise, mankind did not escape sin. But
most of the citizens of Paradise looked to Amos
Burch to lead them to his Promised Land.

Knott's routine varied not at all. Burch scarcely
stopped at Knott's office, and not a word passed between them about any subject other than business.
But the clock was ticking. Knott learned that the
case had been put on Judge Boardman's December
docket; that he would be subpoenaed at the appro-
priate time; that Burch's lawyer, Alden Streeter, was
jousting with Lytell about a change of venue; and

that Streeter was striving, on Burch's behalf, to have the matter summarily dismissed.

"Daniel, Myrtle's case, her freedom, and justice all hinge upon your testimony," Lytell told him.

Knott felt a heavy burden.

In late November two accountants from Denver, Linebarger and Balmain, audited the bank. Knott gave it no thought because it was standard banking practice, and had been done before. But he noted that Burch had chosen a different accounting firm this time. Knott knew the ledgers were in perfect order and there would be no discrepancies.

Hannah grew moody as the civil trial approached and worried more about it than Daniel did.

"It's just a divorce, Hannah," he said one evening.

"Not for Amos Burch. For him it's a dethroning."

Daniel laughed uneasily.

Hannah had abruptly stopped spending money on anything but necessities, and she was keeping some of the family cash in eagles and double eagles hidden in her bread box instead of at the bank. Daniel disapproved. There wasn't much theft in Paradise, but sugar jars and bread boxes were obvious targets.

Thanksgiving arrived, and the Knotts enjoyed a ham with all the trimmings. But Hannah looked strained, and for once, the family gathering seemed taut. The children were noticing, and were asking questions.

"Nothing's wrong, Rosalie," Hannah said, but it erupted as a shout.

"Then why are you always so angry?" Rosalie asked.

December arrived with a storm and a date: the divorce action was scheduled for the fifth. Daniel doubted that he would be employed at Christmas.

"Go lightly on the presents, Hannah," he said. She nodded.

On December 4, Eben Lytell discussed the case with Knott.

"We've requested a jury; they've resisted, wanting a verdict from just their friend Boardman. We've proposed a change of venue to Durango because we believe it will be difficult to get a fair trial in a county where Burch is so prominent and powerful, but they're saying there is no reason to do so. Boardman won't recuse himself. They've won on every point of contention. So we're going before a judge who'll favor his friend Amos as much as he can get away with. That may offer us a chance to appeal later.

"Now, Daniel, simply put, you're our entire case. And for that reason, Streeter's going to try to impeach your testimony. He'll try to establish that Burch wasn't even in the bank that evening. He'll question why you went there at night.

"He'll do everything he can to demonstrate that you're not telling the truth; that maybe you invented the whole story for personal gain—he'll call it blackmail—and he'll try to explain the sudden promotion in the darkest terms.

"I'll help you as best I can during redirect, but

you're in for a rough time. Civil actions are fought ferociously, often harder than criminal actions. My advice is, tell the story just as accurately as you can and don't budge an iota, despite the pressure, the threats, and the scorn that Alden Streeter will throw at you. You're going to feel defiled when he's done. But truth is a shield, and it'll cloak you in the end and deflect the mud."

Daniel swallowed. He had known it would be painful, but now the reality of a trial in which his word would stand against the raging force of a powerful bull seemed terrible to him.

"There's one more thing: they want this trial to be held behind closed doors, no matter what the law of Colorado requires. They argue privacy, prominence, malicious gossip, et cetera, and Boardman has almost, but not quite, gone along with it. He is limiting spectators. This is questionable, and I can file various motions, but mostly after the fact. There is little I can do beforehand."

That did not sound good. Daniel Knott awaited the hour of his testimony as one awaits the guillotine.

Chapter 13

Daniel Knott found himself in the middle of the most painful day of his life. Everything in that courtroom seemed to belong to Amos Burch, who sat granite-faced and unblinking, his gaze boring into Knott.

It was Burch's courthouse. He had led the committee that built it, subscribing a thousand dollars and raising more from his business associates. His word had determined who would preside over the county's business. The elegant austerity of the new stone building expressed Burch's own tastes.

Burch's influence permeated the entire county. He had prodded Paradise toward comfort and elegance. Little remained of the rude crossroads saloon town catering to the cattle drovers and miners in the vicinity, or the rough crowd who had built it. The frontier shantytown had evolved into a glistening gem of a city, a gracious, pleasing, vibrant community aglow with its newness and virtue. In Paradise, life was safe and sweet and smooth.

Behind the judge stood the United States flag along with that of the Centennial State. Beyond the closed door of the courtroom, a sheriff's deputy barred admittance. Within it were only a few people: Judge Boardman, a bailiff, a court recorder, Mrs. Burch, her attorney Eben Lytell, Lytell's own recorder, whom Boardman could find no reason to exclude, Knott, Burch, and his attorney Alden Streeter. The effect was suffocating, and Knott yearned to be outside in the sunlight that streamed through the sole window.

The first part went easily enough: after Knott had been sworn in, Lytell drew the story from him in detail. It was a simple narrative and took little telling. He described what he had witnessed, using delicate language because of Myrtle Burch's presence. Yes, he was positive about who was there. A lamp revealed all. There was no mistake.

Then Lytell drew him through the events that followed including the sudden startling promotion.

"Did Burch give you a reason?"

"Merit, sir."

"Did he offer any other reason?"

"None, sir."

"Did you have a sense of a quid pro quo?"

"I wondered about it."

"Did you wonder what would happen if you declined the promotion?"

"Yes, sir. I feared I would be fired. We're happy in

Paradise, and I didn't want to move my family. I supposed, given Mr. Burch's position here, that if I was fired by the bank, no other positions here would be available to me."

"Did you feel, then, that even though not a word was said about what you had seen, the promotion did have something to do with what had happened?"

"It seemed possible, Mr. Lytell. When I talked it over with my wife, Hannah, we decided that maybe it was based on merit after all. I had done a good job for several years, and I knew everything about bank business but loans. But neither of us was very certain about it. It was a very large raise."

Lytell paused, gathering attention. "After witnessing this act of infidelity, did you at any time entertain the idea of extorting anything from Mr. Burch in exchange for your silence? And did you at any time put such a scheme into effect?"

"No, sir! It never occurred to me. Why would I do that? The raise and promotion came to me unbidden and completely surprised me."

"It was entirely Mr. Burch's initiative?"

"Yes, sir."

Knott saw Streeter writing something down on his pad.

"Did you later have some concrete evidence that a quid pro quo was involved, that your new position was offered in exchange for your silence?"

"Not until this divorce case, sir. I told Mr. Burch that Mrs. Burch and her attorney had been in con-

tact with me and I had told them the story as honestly as I could, and that I intended to testify to it as
accurately as I could."

"And what did Mr. Burch say?"

"He just nodded."

"Did you feel he was inviting you to perjure yourself?" Lytell continued.

"Well, no. He never suggested that. But there was
this idea, sir, about a recommendation and a good
position somewhere else. He talked about that.
When I hesitated to accept the advancement, he told
me to accept it or leave his employment. He did not
allow me to continue in my position as teller."

"He never asked you to falsify your testimony?"

"Never, sir."

"But he did, subtly, pressure you? Hint that
things would not go well for you if you testified accurately?"

Knott dreaded his response. It would bring Amos
Burch to the brink of obstruction of justice. "Yes,
sir," he said. "I kept wondering whether he was trying to obtain my silence."

All the while, Knott felt Burch's unblinking stare
boring into him. It was an odd sensation. There sat
Burch, the soul of moderation, a pillar of civic
virtue, the dashing arbiter of civility and honor in
Paradise, calmly waiting to crush him like some
beetle under a boot.

After a brief recess, it was Alden Streeter's turn.
Knott found himself facing a well-groomed, melan-
choly man in a cutaway, a man who seemed sad-

dened by these weighty proceedings, a man who spoke so quietly and blandly that Knott thought things might go easily for him.

They didn't.

"You wear spectacles, Mr. Knott?"

"For reading."

"Were you wearing spectacles when this alleged event took place?"

"No, sir."

"Would you know Eloise Joiner if you saw her?"

"Yes. She's come into the bank on occasion."

"Was the woman in the office facing you when this alleged discovery happened?"

"No, she, ah, was facing upward."

"But you say you knew who it was?"

"Absolutely."

"Did you look at the rest of her, or only her face?"

Knott felt himself reddening. "Most of the rest of her was not visible, sir. But it was Mrs. Joiner."

"Please answer only the question, sir. A single lamp doesn't produce much light, Mr. Knott, and yet you say you're certain you saw Mr. Burch and Mrs. Joiner. How long did you view this alleged event?"

"Just a moment, sir. I was embarrassed and closed the door."

"Then what happened?"

"I left the building. It was out of courtesy, sir. Until I left, they remained in Mr. Burch's office."

"Does the bank have a custodian?"

"Yes, sir, but it wasn't him."

"Please confine your answers to my questions. We will establish later that Mr. Burch was nowhere near the bank that night. Do you wish to reconsider your sworn testimony?"

"I am telling you exactly what I saw."

"Now, how long had it been since you'd received a raise before this alleged event occurred?"

"Two years, sir."

"And were you unhappy about that?"

"We all hope to progress, Mr. Streeter."

"Answer my question."

"I was not unhappy, but I felt a raise was overdue."

"So there was motive to invent a ridiculous story and use it to extort a raise?"

"That's absurd."

"Is it? All of a sudden you were earning three times your previous salary, and sitting in Mr. Burch's own seat, and fulfilling Mr. Burch's own duties. That's what you always wanted, eh?"

"I never dreamed of it, sir, and I resent the implication that—"

Boardman's gavel rapped sharply. "The witness will subside," he said.

Knott felt the heat rise. "Your Honor, this man is trying to make me out to be an extortionist. It's a lie!"

"You are close to contempt, Knott," Boardman said.

Knott choked back his anger.

All that long and brutal morning in the courthouse in Paradise, Alden Streeter probed and needled and whittled at Daniel Knott's testimony, and all that while Knott doggedly clung to his story.

During the lunch recess, Knott discovered he had a headache, and his body felt as if he had gone ten rounds with a prizefighter.

But during the redirect that afternoon, Lytell opened doors for Knott.

"Do you expect retribution from Mr. Burch for this testimony?" he asked.

"I fear it, but hope it won't happen, sir. Mr. Burch has always upheld the highest ideals. I hope truthful testimony would not be a reason to dismiss me."

"Objection. Not germane. Where is this leading?" Streeter piped up.

"Mr. Knott is explaining his motives, which came under assault this morning, Your Honor."

Boardman paused, then allowed the line of questioning to continue.

"Mr. Knott, when I first talked with you about the case and told you that Mrs. Burch and I needed your testimony to verify what we suspected, which was that you had some knowledge of adultery, and I raised the question of whether Mr. Burch had attempted to obtain your silence by preemptively elevating you to this town's elite—"

"Objection!" Streeter interrupted again.

"Mr. Lytell, that line is out of bounds," the judge said.

"—you volunteered what you knew, after a night of thinking about it. Why did you do that?"

"Truth and justice, sir. Truth is sacred to me. And it became clear to me from what you said that Mrs. Burch had become a neglected woman—"

"Objection," said Streeter once again.

"Sustained," said Boardman. "Strike that."

But Daniel Knott had been given his moment. He was excused soon after, and the divorce suit proceeded behind closed doors. The Colorado Livery Stable hostler, Billy Quaid, was waiting in the corridor, and Knott had a hunch that Quaid would be testifying about Mrs. Joiner's comings and goings, and no doubt Amos's as well. Maybe Quaid's testimony would support his own. But Knott doubted that he would ever know. This whole case was a ghostly presence floating unseen through Paradise.

Knott walked to his house and collapsed on his bed for a while. Hannah sat silently beside him and asked nothing. Then Daniel Knott returned to work.

Chapter 14

The rest of the day proceeded in eerie silence. Knott studied some pending loans, ascertaining if they could be collateralized, amid a quietness that belied the veiled drama going on over in the stone courthouse.

He heard not a shred of gossip. No customer alluded to the divorce; no other bank employee was even aware of it. The *Tattler* reported only good news. No one at the courthouse was talking—not when their livelihoods and reputations depended on the favor of the town's leading light.

Plainly, the town of Paradise knew nothing of the divorce trial, on scandalous ground, of its leading light and moral paragon. And that, obviously, was how Amos Burch intended to keep matters.

Knott watched the clock tick past three, closing time at the Merchant Bank, and then past six, when his colleagues had completed their tallies and left.

Burch never appeared. The firing that Knott had waited for all day, making his stomach churn and his heart thump and press against his chest, wasn't going to happen—at least not just then. But Knott was not fooled.

He turned down the lamps and watched them blue out and smoke, then armored himself against the chill of the evening, locking the door behind him as he left. Would Burch forgive him? Was not his honest testimony proof of his integrity; proof that Knott would be a reliable and rock-solid banker all his life? Yes, that was the way to look at it: Burch was a large-spirited man and would see Knott's good character in the testimony.

Knott found Hannah kneading bread dough in the kitchen. She searched his face, expecting the worst, and not finding it, kissed him lightly.

"No, not fired today," Knott said. "I think we'll be all right. Amos Burch is a grand man, actually. Everything he's done for this town . . ."

"I am not so sure," Hannah interrupted.

Daniel grinned. "I'm not either. But here we are— I still have a job, and we're still planning on a happy life in Paradise."

"Tell me how it went," she said.

He told her about Alden Streeter's ruthless effort to undermine Knott's testimony; even going so far as to seek out motives for hurting Mr. Burch.

"But I never once budged, Hannah. Not once did he push me into saying something untrue. I'm a stubborn cuss. It just isn't in me to do that."

She sighed. "We'll pay a price. But Daniel, don't worry. I'm proud of you. Even if we're forced to move, even if you get fired, I'll stand beside you. You did what you had to do, and I would do the same thing if I had to testify. Daniel, that's why we are together. You and I against the world."

She drew his hand into hers and squeezed it.

My God, what a woman!

He felt so lucky. How many women would support their husbands even if it meant losing a job, income, and a good life in a town they enjoyed? How many would understand? How many would instead urge their men to make a few small compromises for the sake of the family, the children, the next meal?

He didn't sleep well. The next morning he detoured to the home of Eben Lytell, hoping for news. He found the attorney in his parlor-office, studying a casebook.

"Ah, come in, Daniel. I've been meaning to contact you. Your testimony was excellent. You couldn't be shaken loose. If Mrs. Burch wins, it'll be because of your testimony. There simply are no other grounds. I think we dealt with questions of motive by preemptively raising the issue. What you conveyed to the court was simply that yes, Burch wanted your silence and tried to secure it with the promotion, but he stopped short of anything illegal or improper. That's just what I hoped to establish. It shifts the whole issue away from malice or blackmail on your part. And it clears Burch of anything other than a wish to hush it all up."

"Yes, well, what was the decision?"

"There's none yet. Streeter moved to postpone the rest of it for a week; said he'll present new evidence. I can't imagine what. That's all I can tell you; everything's under seal, you know."

"I saw Billy Quaid in the corridor after I left. I guess he was your witness."

Lytell grinned and said nothing.

"Well, at least tell me when it'll be over."

Lytell shrugged.

Knott sighed. "I haven't been fired, if you want to know my status."

"You expected to be?"

Knott nodded.

Lytell looked unusually sober. "I think you'll know Amos Burch's frame of mind after the trial ends—but not before. If he fires you for anything but cause, he is going to be on precarious ground. I admire your courage."

"If it weren't for Hannah, I couldn't do it."

He left the lawyer's office with little more information than he had before. But he did learn one thing: it was far from over. The Burches remained married, for the moment.

He let himself into the bank, walking past Miss Gustafson, who was busy writing statements, and entered his office, surprised to find the lamp lit. He was not surprised to discover Burch, but the others present puzzled him. They included the two outside auditors from Denver and Mark St. John, one of the bank's directors.

"Come in, Knott, and close the door," Burch said. The man looked like a thundercloud ready to storm. Knott knew instantly that he was in big trouble.

"My auditors, Mr. Linebarger and Mr. Balmain, have discovered some accounting irregularities— and I use the phrase delicately—in your ledgers. These end abruptly in June, immediately after you were elevated to your present position."

Knott felt a hot red fear thread through him. "Sir! That couldn't be true! I have always kept accurate—"

"Nine thousand seven hundred dollars peculated, Knott. Almost ten thousand dollars lost to the depositors at Merchant Bank."

"Sir! That is not possible!"

"They have traced it to you, Knott. Two dummy accounts; all deposit information written in your hand. A simple, ingenious scheme, Daniel. You simply added a quarter percent to the interest rate on loans and mortgages. If the mortgage contract called for eight percent compound interest, you simply began a ledger listing eight and a quarter percent as the interest, and employed the actuarial tables to record each payment—at the higher interest rate—and pocketed the profit. Small change, but it added up fast in your dummy accounts. Here it all is, in your own handwriting.

"Look at this contract. Here, it's six and three-quarters percent interest. But look in your ledger, and the actuarial tables. It's listed as seven percent. Ah, what could be easier? And who would discover it? Every entry correct, so long as the wrong rate is employed to calculate the interest. As for the dummy accounts, held by people unknown in Paradise, the withdrawals are all in cash." He stared. "Utterly simple. You've robbed the borrowers and the bank."

"Let me see!"

"Have a good look."

St. John thrust a loan ledger before Knott. There, indeed, were accounts in Knott's own hand.

"I want to study these. And the contracts."

"You're welcome to work with the accountants' duplicates and workups. But you're going to be indicted unless you come up with an explanation."

"In court?"

"Of course. Judge Boardman's district court. Embezzlers are brought before the bar, are they not? I've placed Mark St. John in charge of the matter."

A dark cloud of suspicion settled on Knott. "If you think I'm guilty, why are you waiting?"

"To give you a chance to prove you didn't do it."

Knott felt his pulse race. He could scarcely fathom any of this, with prison and disgrace now looming like an ominous specter over his head. "I am innocent, sir! There's obviously a mistake. I've never taken a penny from the bank!"

"We'll see," St. John said. "If you can prove to our satisfaction that you're innocent, why, all will be forgotten."

"How can I do that?"

"We'll give you a few hours to think it over."

"Think it over? I don't have anything to think over."

"Yes, you do, Knott. Amos asked that you have time to think it over."

"I'll need to see the ledgers. How can I prove to you that I'm innocent if I can't see the books and the loan contracts? I just want to compare the rates specified in the contracts with the rates in the ledgers."

"That's exactly what our outside auditors did, Knott. It's an airtight case." He smiled with a thin malignant levity. "If you cooperate fully with us— and I mean *fully*, Knott—Amos Burch might be lenient. That's what he tells me. He knows how hard it is to raise a family on so little."

"What are you talking about?"

"Mr. Burch is a charitable man. That is one of the many reasons he's so admired here. He's also a forgiving one. He won't take this to the sheriff for criminal action, or press civil suit, unless you give him no choice. You let us know by morning, all right?"

"But—"

"Here are the accountants' workups. See whether you can find fault with them."

"But I need the original contracts!"

"Let us know first thing in the morning, Knott."

"But—"

Burch herded the others out of Knott's office, leaving Daniel to wrestle alone with his nightmare.

He sagged into his chair, the weight of events crushing his chest until he could barely breathe. He had taken nothing, not one dime! He couldn't steal if he tried! He thought he knew what had been done: it wasn't the ledgers that had been doctored by someone, it was the loan and mortgage contracts, which now bore rates and terms different from those he had carefully listed in the ledgers. Who had done it, and why? And how could it be done without the consent of the borrowers, who all had their own copies of the original loan agreements?

What did they mean, *cooperate*?

The answer boiled up in his soul instantly. Find some way to recant, to impeach his own testimony, and the trumped-up charge would be dropped, and he would probably be allowed to resign and escape Paradise. Stick to the truth, and he would face felony grand theft.

Chapter 15

Hannah Knott sat tensely on the edge of the bed, hearing awful words cascade in tormented bursts from Daniel. *Grand theft, embezzlement, trial, prison.* She could barely stand his desperation, and wanted to cry out for him to stop. But there was no stopping this bleak story.

"But, Daniel, you didn't do it! I know you didn't. It's not even in you to do it."

"I have no proof."

"What can you do?"

"Figure out what someone did to the books. Those were my own figures they showed me. I know my hand. So it has to be something else. I thought maybe they'd altered the loan contracts, but I don't see how because there's two copies, and one is in the hands of the borrowers. I can't figure out what those new accountants did."

"But why did they do it, Daniel?"

He swallowed slowly. He looked to be on the brink of collapse, as though he were carrying more than any mortal could possibly carry.

"Amos."

He sighed. She clutched his hand, which was clammy.

"They haven't gone to the sheriff yet. They didn't send the law to arrest me. They're waiting. I guess that's the whole story. Do you see what I mean? *They're waiting.*"

She didn't fathom what he was talking about. "Why would Amos Burch do this? He's put such confidence in you, Daniel."

"You know, Hannah. We both know."

"No, I don't know."

"He wants me to recant my testimony in the divorce case. Or else he'll ruin me."

"Would he go that far?"

He stared at her from a face so bleak that it broke her heart. "You were right about him. I saw only the mask. I didn't realize he would feel so threatened by exposure."

"But he can't do this! All you have to do is tell the judge."

Daniel shook his head. "About what? The bank people never said a word about the divorce, and there were four of them to corroborate each other. Four witnesses against one. They didn't ask me to recant, or perjure, or lie. They didn't even hint at it."

"Then how do you know that's what they want you to do?"

"I just know, that's all."

"What are you going to do?"

Daniel shook his head. "I don't know. I'm so scared I can't think. I know one thing. This isn't about embezzlement. It's about shutting me up. All I have to do is sell my soul. Recant my testimony for whatever reason I choose. Pretend I didn't see Mrs. Joiner and Amos Burch. Just correct my testimony a little, say it was too dark for me to see who was in that office. Then they won't press the embezzlement charge. They'll still fire me and hustle me out of town, but I'll be free. That's why they gave me time to think it over. Time to turn myself into a liar. Time to save my skin."

"You can't prove they're twisting your arm?"

"No."

"What will become of you? Of us?"

He whispered. "If I stick to my story in the divorce case, they'll charge me with grand theft and then convict me and send me to jail. They'll take away everything we possess. The house, furniture, everything in this kitchen, all but the clothing on our backs. Everything! You and the children will be destitute and without a husband and father. Paupers, living in rags, begging, doing menial labor. How will you survive? As a serving girl in a saloon? You and the children will face shame and disgrace, and it will twist their lives and hurt you so much that you'll hardly dare show your face in Paradise. And that's just the beginning. For me, it's the end of my life. Even on the day I walk out of prison, I won't have a future. No job, no hope. When they steal hope from you, they steal the last treasure we possess . . . except honor."

"Amos Burch would do that to you?"

"He's giving me a choice."

"He can't steal what's inside of you, Dan. You can still hold your head high. Inside yourself, you know what is true. They can't steal that."

"I think they'll try to steal even that."

"You've got to talk to people! You've got to tell everyone! You've got to throw light on this!"

He shook his head. "What good would that do? Everyone in Paradise would just take it for the babbling of a crook desperate to cover his crime with a lot of wild excuses."

"Please, Daniel, don't fight this alone."

He stared out the window into the blackness. "I'll talk to Mrs. Burch's lawyer. I don't think he'll help, though. He can't. His task is to get his client the divorce she's seeking. Now his prize witness is about to be indicted. He'll just tell me to see another lawyer."

"Then do it!"

"In Paradise?"

He was right. The other lawyers in private practice were Alden Streeter and Mark St. John, both of them thick with Burch.

"Daniel, I've never been so scared."

"I just feel helpless. I'm only one man, and Amos Burch has everything on his side. Wealth, power, the sheriff, the town constables, the court, the paper, the leading citizens, the best lawyers. Everything. I can't even get my testimony, or my side of the story, into the *Tattler*. I can't even find a lawyer to defend me. I'm all alone."

"No, you're not," she said softly.

The brutal reality was sinking in, and Hannah saw little hope. Why was Amos Burch doing this? What difference did it make if he had been caught with Mrs. Joiner? Other people make mistakes and survive them. He could survive this. But he chose to bury it, discrediting his wife, defeating her suit, going to any lengths to preserve the benign face he presented to the world.

"It's the children I'm worried about," she said.

He nodded. If their father was a convicted thief, and in jail, their lives would be hopelessly twisted. He knew that, and she saw the agony in him when she brought it up.

"I wish to God I had never seen them," he said.

"Maybe pleading to God is a good idea," she said.

He gripped her hand. "That's all we have."

She didn't sleep but lay rigid as a board in bed that night. He wasn't sleeping either, and his tossing about was driving her mad. She finally threw off the comforter, dug her toes into her slippers, found her wrapper on its peg, and hurried down the stairs in the moonless dark until she reached the kitchen, still slightly warm from the residue of the fire in the kitchen range.

She scratched a lucifer, lit the coal-oil lamp, and replaced the glass chimney. She drew water from the reservoir in the range, hoping it would still be hot. It wasn't, but it hadn't cooled down to room temperature, either. It would do. She poured some tea into a strainer and dipped it into the tepid water, using the little rituals to avoid thinking about the disaster that they confronted.

The children. Oh, God, some brute force in the universe was about to tear their small, tender lives to shreds. She withdrew the strainer and sipped at the tea.

She soon heard the padding of his slippers and knew he was as restless as she. The seven-day clock was at two, but their lives were stuck on midnight.

She offered him tea, but he shook his head and slumped into a chair at the battered kitchen table, rubbing his face. She heard the sharp acrimonious whir of his hands scraping his bristly chin.

"It's the children I'm worried about," she said. "Isn't there some way to avoid this?"

He stopped rubbing his face.

"Just this once?" she asked.

"What are you saying?"

"Is your pride worth it? Do you really know what you're doing to this family?"

He seemed to draw into himself, as if she weren't there. "Yes," he said at last. "It isn't pride, Hannah."

"Can't you compromise? You'll hurt all of us, yourself worst of all. What is prison really like? Day after day after day?"

Slowly he shook his head, like a prizefighter who'd just been punched.

"There's got to be a way for the sake of the chil-dren."

"What? Tell Judge Boardman that I lied under oath?"

"No, just sort of correct it. Just say you're not really sure it was Amos in there."

"But I *am* sure. Please don't ask me to—"

"Yes, I am asking you! I'm asking you for us, for Peter and Rosalie and Daniel. For me, because you love me. For yourself, so you don't condemn your-self to disgrace. So you don't toss away your one mortal life, and us along with it!"

She saw his face crumple, but she didn't relent.

"I know it's hard, Dan, but you've responsibili-ties. You've a family. In a week you'll forget it."

"No, if I did that, I'd never forget it."

"But God'll forgive you! He forgives anything if you just ask!"

"I wouldn't be able to forgive myself."

"Are you more holy than God?"

"No, Hannah. I'm just a regular man."

"Please think of us."

The sad stare of his eyes rebuked her, and she felt bad.

"I'm not good at lying," he said.

He ran his hands through his hair as if he could find some sort of solace in the motion. But there was nothing to placate him, and she ached because he was being torn to shreds, and she was tormenting him.

"I'm sorry," she said.

"People who do the right thing, and resist temptation, are supposed to come out all right. That's what you always hear in church. But this won't come out all right, not against a man like Amos Burch."

She couldn't argue with that. "At least talk to Eben Lytell," she said. "He's a lawyer, and maybe he can do things we don't know about."

"Sure, and maybe he'll believe I did steal the bank's money."

The tea had gone bitter on her tongue. She deposited her cup and saucer on the drainboard and stalked up to the darkened bedroom. She knew he would spend the rest of this night in the kitchen, his soul and his heart at war.

Chapter 16

Before dawn, Knott shaved and dressed quietly, bundled himself against the autumnal chill, and plunged into the dark world. He had not slept, and wondered whether he would ever sleep again. He strode north purposefully, his destination a certain foothill ridge where he could behold the rising sun to the east and the gold-burnished wall of the San Juans to the north and west. He had taken this half hour walk many times, especially when he needed perspective.

From there, he would see the peaceful village resting sleepily in its valley, and the affairs of mere mortals would shrink to inconsequence. From that ridge he could fathom the eternal things, the everlasting goodness of the universe. From there he might separate things of value from cheaper coinage. From there, he hoped, he might come to a decision.

For this was a desert place, a place of communion with his Creator.

He struggled along through the blackness, stumbling now and then on unseen snares, yet intuitively knowing how to reach his destination—and perhaps his destiny. He was winded when he reached the top, for the trail upward rose steeply in spots, just like life's journey. All across the east and southeast a rim of blue announced the coming day. But at his back, the mountains loomed gloomy and foreboding. He loved this place.

In his mind, love fought with duty, truth with falsehood, honor with cravenness. He settled onto a boulder, his back to the sharp breeze that cut through his clothing just as reality cuts through the wool of fantasy and delusion.

He worried most about his sons. The sins of fathers somehow afflicted sons more than daughters. How would Peter and Daniel Junior fare in Paradise if their father were convicted of embezzlement and sent to the state penitentiary? Dear Rosalie would survive; girls were blessedly immune. But neighbor children would pick on Peter and poor little Daniel, taunt them cruelly, label them sons of a jailbird. And poverty would shrink their small lives down to nothing, forcing them to wear rags, and to grow up without the loving attention of a mother who would have to toil twelve hours a day at washing, or cleaning, or some other menial tasks.

Could he inflict that on them just for the sake of his vanity? Who would know, after all, if he politely

recanted his testimony, lying just a little bit to spare
his own flesh and blood the brutal consequences?
Only he would know; only his own self-esteem
would suffer. Even Hannah, in the end, had asked
him to spare her and the family the ordeal they
faced. All it would take was a minor amendment of
his testimony. All he had to say was that, on reflection, he could not be sure who it was that he saw.

But he was sure.

All he would achieve by sticking to his testimony
was to uphold his honor. All he would do, at bottom, was be able to tell himself that he hadn't sold
his soul. And it was just as Hannah said: God would
surely forgive him for trying to protect his family,
for loving his children and his wife so much that he
would do whatever it took to spare them misery. He
worshiped a forgiving God; that lay at the heart of
his belief. So why should he resist doing what he
needed to do, what could be viewed as an act of sacrifice and love?

But it wouldn't be just—not quite. His small re-
cantation would deny Myrtle Burch the freedom
and compensation to which she surely was entitled.
It would cheapen justice in Archuleta County. A
small, foul lie would decorate its trial records. But
that lie would preserve himself and his family, restore life in Paradise to what it was. Though Myrtle
Burch would remain married, she would be comforted by wealth.

He didn't even care much about Myrtle Burch.
She had everything, or at least every material thing.

He didn't doubt that he, Daniel Knott, was the richer mortal by far. He was loved. Maybe that was all the more reason to be just; to stick to the truth. Myrtle Burch was the impoverished one, not he.

The sky quickened in the east, and the blue gave way to white and then gold, and he knew the blazing orb lay just below the horizon. Off to the west, the San Juans began to glow with the dawn.

How small Paradise looked below him. Smoke now eddied from the morning fires of a hundred cookstoves as women began heating their ranges for breakfast. He looked down upon a city whose lord was one man; his word was law, his benevolences nurtured the poor, his enlightened charity and mild discipline contained crime. He fostered religion, provided jobs, ensured a stable economy, encouraged progress. One man, gifted with utopian visions. A good man, dreaming of a perfect world.

But now a man willing to employ the most ruthless and brutal tactics merely to preserve his reputation. After all, his reputation is all a man has. Take away a man's good name, and what is left of him? How acutely that truth pressed on Knott. With a small lie, Knott could preserve his own reputation, that of his family, and Amos Burch's as well.

But was anyone's reputation worth a small injustice?

The sun blinded him, and now he beheld the San Juan Mountains, mysterious and ever present, the source of water and minerals and timber for Paradise. The mountains would be there long after

Daniel Knott and Amos Burch had vanished from the earth. There was right and there was wrong, and Daniel knew he could only do right, and pray God for mercy for doing right.

He realized, suddenly, that his mind was made up. He dreaded what was to follow. He realized that this would probably be the last sunrise he would see as a free man . . . at least for ten or fifteen years. He looked lovingly upon it. The cloudless heavens, the great panorama that spread before him, the freedom in every direction. Tomorrow he would peer through bars.

He paused to thank God. He had sometimes wrestled with God, sometimes doubted. But this morning he saw God everywhere in the universe and its orderly design, and saw good and evil as the eternal lodestones. He was not comforted. He would soon be saying good-bye to his very own family.

He needed to get to work, and so he started down the long, twisted path into a twisted world. He walked straight to work, standing erect and stiff, like a man walking to the gallows, determined not to show the world his terror.

He was late. Jasper Pickering had already opened the Merchant Bank. The new teller, Adah Wainwright, was at her window. Knott nodded, then headed into his office and waited. He focused on the positive: maybe this entire embezzlement business was an error that would be exposed. Maybe it really did have nothing to do with the divorce trial.

Maybe virtue would be rewarded: nothing evil would befall him. Was it not true that evil men flee when no one pursues them? He had done no wrong; he did not need to flee.

At last, in his office, his sleepless body rebelled, and he wondered how he could endure the long day. He noticed a stack of documents in manila folders and realized he had been so distraught that he hadn't even examined what lay before his eyes. The material proved to be the "evidence" against him. One stack consisted of loan and mortgage contracts, and the other stack consisted of the bank ledger pages recording the payments. For years he had recorded these payments, usually made semi-annually or annually. With each payment from a borrower, he had consulted the actuarial tables and recorded the gross payment, the amount of interest, and the amount of principal remaining to be paid down.

At the top of each ledger page was a notation: the borrower's name and address, the date of the contract's issue, the bank number assigned to the contract, and the rate of interest. All in his hand. He perused these against the contracts and discovered, in each case, that the agreed-upon interest in the contract was a half or a quarter percent lower than in his ledger. The sight filled him with horror. He could not explain it. He examined the ledgers for each of the dummy accounts and discovered transfers of small amounts that corresponded to the amounts skimmed out of the loans by recording more interest than provided by the contracts.

The finger pointed directly at him. He studied the dozen contracts for signs of tampering and could fine none. The only thing that bothered him was that the contracts seemed too clean, too new, too little handled for bank papers that were withdrawn from file drawers, piled on his desk, and examined several times a year. If the contracts were forged—and he suspected they were—he would have his answer.

But who had done it, and why?

He thought he knew: those new auditors from Denver did it; and they did it for Amos Burch. And they were to be the lever Burch had over Knott, either to get him to recant his testimony or to impeach it altogether as the unreliable word of a thief. But not in a million years could Daniel Knott prove it.

He grew aware of someone standing at the door, and when he looked up he beheld the attorney Mark St. John, crony and confidant of Amos Burch and director of the Merchant Bank.

"Well, Knott?" he asked blandly.

"These are not the original contracts, not the ones I dealt with," Knott said.

"And you can prove this?"

"Maybe. But the borrowers have duplicates. We can see if they match."

"I hear the maundering of a guilty man, perhaps?"

"No, I have never taken one cent from this bank."

"Oh, come now, Knott. It's all there before your eyes. We know the facts. Now, have you decided to come clean?"

"What do you mean, come clean?"

St. John smiled, shrugged slightly. "Amos says that he'll be easy on you if you'll cooperate. He expressly asked me to tell you that. He's a mild man, Knott. Always forgiving of human frailty."

Knott turned cold inside and felt ice gather around his heart. "This alleged embezzlement is a fraud, and you know it. It's simply a threat to hold over me. It hasn't a thing to do with the bank, but with my testimony at Amos Burch's divorce trial."

"What on earth are you talking about, Knott?"

"The divorce that is now being tried before Judge Boardman, in which Mrs. Burch alleged adultery. I am her witness."

"Are you daft?"

Knott saw no reason to reply. The lawyer was being disingenuous, pretending not to know of the case his partner was defending. The moment stretched, and Knott decided to end it.

"I will not lie," he snapped. "I will not recant my testimony. I saw Mr. Burch and Mrs. Joiner, and no other, in an intimate embrace. There was no mistake. You will not get me to go before Judge Boardman and have Alden Streeter lead me through a lie. I will not stoop to your level."

"My goodness, Knott, you're demented. What has that action to do with embezzlement?"

"Go! Go tell Amos Burch that he can destroy me, but he can't break my honor."

"Isn't this a bit melodramatic? Quite some rhetoric from an embezzler. Let's see, that particular felony—grand theft—can run five to fifteen years."

"You cannot break me. I have told the truth and I will stick to it."

"An odd assertion from an employee accused of embezzlement, Knott. I'll give you an hour or so more to think things over, but only because Amos wants to give you as much rope as possible. But I'm afraid that I'll have to file a complaint after lunch, and you'll face both criminal and civil actions. That is, unless you can exculpate yourself."

The threat hung there, dirty and shameful.

"You're adept at not saying what you mean to say. You are inviting me to tell a lie on Burch's behalf or face ruin. I don't know much law, but I know you're suborning a witness, and what you're doing is itself a felony."

St. John looked genuinely horrified. "You are utterly stupid, Knott. It would be criminal malfeasance on my part to do such a thing. Keep your delusions to yourself."

"Go!" Knott yelled, rage breaking through.

Chapter 17

Amos Burch listened impatiently to Mark St. John in the upstairs suite. He didn't particularly like the man, who had a dandruff problem so severe that the shoulders of his dark suits sometimes resembled snowcapped ridges. But he suppressed his disgust. In a frontier town one made do with whatever material was at hand.

"Are you sure Knott understood?"

"Absolutely."

"How do you know?"

"Knott spelled it out and accused me of suborning perjury. I told him that was absurd. The very accusation angers me! He puts on a great front, one of pure indignation. I assured him you would prosecute a remedy in a civil suit and file criminal charges."

"He denied his guilt, I suppose."

"Vehemently. The trouble is, he's ready to immolate himself on some private altar or another."

They were treading delicate ground. Not even his friend St. John knew that the "embezzlement" was Burch's own concoction. There were things lawyers shouldn't know, and Burch intended to keep his own secrets. The outside auditors didn't know, either. He had brought them in expressly to discover something amiss. Burch himself had redone the ledgers and set up the dummy accounts that pointed a finger at Daniel Knott. It was not hard to copy Knott's neat, orderly hand.

It was a pity he had to do it. The whole business was distasteful in the extreme, and it troubled Burch. He certainly did not wish to suborn a witness; all that was required was the slightest modification of Knott's recollections. Not a lie, really, just an admission of confusion or doubt. If Knott admitted, under oath, that he wasn't really sure who was in the office, Burch's old friend and penny-ante poker pal Judge Boardman would end the case swiftly. But Knott's uncompromising testimony stood like a boulder in the path of Burch's hopes. He sighed. How strange was fate.

Amos Burch recoiled from the very measures he had taken to defend himself. He knew himself to be, at bottom, a good and moral man. And here he was, resorting to things he had never dreamed he would do as a last resort, only to defeat an obdurate and foolish young man who could not be bent in the slightest. He felt dyspeptic. Why were his innards roiling so?

This town had all been Burch's doing, his utopian vision, his gentle guidance of Paradise into a haven of prosperity, safety, and progress. This was America! Burch saw himself as a patriot, fashioning a splendid new civilization out of a wilderness inhabited only by wandering tribes. He was an artist, and Colorado was his canvas. Someday the whole world would understand what he had wrought in this virgin valley.

But now, this one time, he would have to violate his own rules for the sake of the community. He felt himself walking along the edge of an abyss. If he should fall, there would be no bottom. He would plunge to his doom. His reputation and the admiration that surrounded him were more precious than life itself. He would rather die than tumble into sordid disgrace.

Mark St. John had every reason to believe that the embezzlement was real. He trusted Burch implicitly when Burch had told him the young man had stolen substantial amounts in a clever scheme that involved interest-rate manipulation. The lawyer had always been zealous in his protection of the Merchant Bank.

St. John was now looking at him expectantly, wanting direction.

Burch sighed. Now he would cross the Rubicon, though he hated it. "All right. File a complaint. Go fetch the sheriff. And file the replevin, and don't forget to attach every bit of property Knott possesses. It won't cover the bank's loss, but every penny counts."

St. John nodded and hastened down the long stairwell to street level. Burch watched him from his upstairs window. He felt melancholic. Why had fate deserted him now? He was an honorable man, forced by tawdry circumstance to do something utterly out of bounds. Better that one man be sacrificed than that the whole town be torn to bits.

It was not anyone's fault. Well, yes, perhaps it was. Myrtle lay at the bottom of it. Her unceasing demands on his time, her arthritis, her increasing unhappiness had all driven him into the arms of Eloise. Ah, Lord, what a blessing that was. In all his life, he had never known so vibrant a woman, so joyous a lover as Eloise. Surely God himself had brought them together and given them their private Eden. He decided impulsively to go visit her. They had stayed apart during the opening phase of the divorce action, but now, with the case recessed for a while, he would just slip out there.

He didn't want to be around when they hauled Knott away, didn't want to suffer Knott's accusations. He didn't doubt that Knott would blabber to anyone and everyone, and the quickest way to quiet all that talk was not respond. The *Tattler* would report nothing. Sheriff Kennear and his deputies would say not a word.

He wished, sadly, that Knott had bent a little, even just an inch. Then everything would be fine, and he would not now be suffering this hollow feeling in his belly. Knott enraged him. What was the matter with the man? He deserved his fate. He would cause his own wife and children to suffer, and that disgusted Burch. What sort of man would not even protect his family? What sort of world was Knott living in?

Burch had his horse and buggy brought around, and by midmorning was driving briskly up the valley road in a cloudless and cold day. He eyed the pastures with interest; the condition of the cattle always intrigued him. The distant snowcapped San Juans beckoned to him. Pine forests blanketed their flanks, a fortune to be taken at the right moment, when the market for wood was ripe. Even now, he was quietly buying up patented forest land and negotiating with the government for whatever he could get.

That was how to get ahead. Pasture had value. Water had value. Trees and minerals had value. There, within sight, lay a millionaire's wildest dream. That was what America was about: getting rich!

He drove through sere pastures, slumbering before the wrath of winter; he studied the fat Shorthorn cattle, which flourished in this country. He steered his prized dray horse around long pools of muck, the result of good autumnal rains. This was a sweet land and he rejoiced in it. It was almost all his own.

An hour later he pulled into Eloise's yard and

hooked El Morocco's bridle to a carriage weight. It was not yet noon, and he was brimming with anticipation of a good lunch and a tryst with the loveliest of women. He knocked, but was not rewarded with a response, and eventually found her in her garden. She was pulling up cornstalks and cleaning away debris for the winter.

"Why, Amos!"

He embraced her, as he always did, and felt an odd resistance in her.

"I sneaked away. We've the whole afternoon, Eloise. Just to ourselves."

She didn't respond to that with her usual joy. "All right," she said. "I suppose you'd like lunch."

"You are the world's best cook."

"Amos, you flatter me. I am an average cook. There was never time to learn how to be a good cook, and I scarcely bother at all now that I am widowed."

He was taken aback. This was an Eloise he had not seen before. He followed her to the pump, where she washed her hands, and then into the kitchen, which was pleasantly warm. She threw wood into the range and then led him to the front parlor, decorated with cheap mail-order dark oak furniture and some Audubon lithographs on the wall. The Joiners had never had anything to spare.

"Things are changing, Eloise. Changing at the bank. We're having a little unpleasantness there. A trusted employee—well, I'll spare you the details."

"You've been sparing me the details of your divorce."

"Of course, to protect you."

"Protect me?" She plainly was bewildered.

"Why, Eloise, you are my one and only love, and I don't even want you to think of Myrtle."

"But I do, Amos. Why are you fighting her? You've told me fifty times you'd been unhappy in your marriage. I thought you *wanted* a divorce!"

"Why, she's asking too much, that's all."

She stared bleakly at him. "Amos, you've led me to think all these months that if only you could get free of Myrtle, you would make me yours. That, of all things on this good earth, marriage to me was your ideal, your bliss, you uttermost hope."

He saw where this was leading and hoped to head it off.

"I would, and I will someday. But you see, Myrtle's making a fuss. On principle, I must resist."

"What sort of fuss?"

"Oh, that's something I'd rather not go into. Judge Boardman has sealed the proceedings so I can't talk about it. Not a word."

She laughed bitterly, which astonished him. She was unhappy; it was written all over her face. "You still haven't answered my question," she said. "Why don't you let Myrtle go? Do you really want to make me your wife, Amos? Are your promises to me something I should forget?"

"I desperately want you for my wife, Eloise. You are the most sublime woman—"

"Yes," she said quietly. "You've told me that a thousand times. But when it comes to sharing your life, your thoughts, your divorce, your problems with Myrtle, you build walls."

"Eloise—"

"I will heat some end-of-the-garden stew for lunch," she said. "Then I want answers to my questions. Things are happening that I don't know about. If we are to be lovers and friends, Amos, there must be no walls."

Her soft gaze did not hide something steely behind it.

He didn't like that at all.

Chapter 18

So they were still giving him time to make a liar of himself. One more hour. Daniel Knott huddled at his desk, the cold fingers of dread pressing upon him. He could still stop this. A simple one-minute walk to Alden Streeter's law office would do it.

He cursed himself for being so stupid. What would his rectitude get him but disgrace, the ruin of his family, poverty, the torment of his wife and children—and years in the state penitentiary?

But in the midst of his terror lay his strength: he believed in right and wrong, good and evil, and the love of a transcendent God. They might destroy his life and body, but they would not destroy the inner light that illumined his every act.

He stared at the pile of incriminating documents. He knew better than to destroy them. Burch was practically inviting him to shove all those papers into the coal stove. Then they would truly have him.

He itched to flee, gather his wife and children, buy a wagon and run away to New Mexico, not far away. But the sheriff would overtake him in an hour.

Wearily—he wondered whether he could even find the strength to walk a few blocks—he rose, clambered into his coat, and braved the sharp wind. A five-minute hike took him to the home and office of Eben Lytell. This time, Daniel was coming for his own sake, and not to further someone else's cause. He entered, sat in the foyer that served as a reception area, and waited. Lytell did not appear. The lawyer's door was open, so Knott peered in. Lytell was not present.

Knott wondered what to do. Small decisions had suddenly become perversely difficult. He decided to wait. Let them find him here. This is where the sheriff would come anyway if Knott could not be found at the bank or in his home. Here, where his troubles had begun. He wished Myrtle Burch and Eben Lytell had never put together a theory about the string of events that led to his promotion, and had never required his testimony. If he had not been forced to testify, he would still be living peaceably with his family. He raged at Lytell for driving him to this, and yet he could go to no other lawyer in Paradise.

It was well past noon of that fateful day before Lytell wandered in. He seemed surprised to find Knott there. He hung his coat on a hall tree, and nodded Knott into his parlor-office.

"Well, Daniel?" he asked.

"I'm in trouble."

This time Lytell looked him over, obviously drawing conclusions. Knott knew he looked haggard after yet another sleepless night filled with hours of torment.

"I'm about to be arrested."

Lytell's eyebrow arched.

"For grand theft. Embezzlement."

"How do you know this?"

"Yesterday the documents were laid before me at the bank."

"By whom?"

"Mr. Burch, two auditors from Denver, and Mark St. John."

"And what are you accused of?"

"Overcharging borrowers with slightly higher interest than the contracts specified and pocketing the difference in dummy accounts."

Lytell said nothing, waiting.

"I didn't do it!" The words exploded from Knott like shrapnel.

Lytell stared into the sunlight outside. "And then what happened?"

"They invited me to cooperate. Said it would go lighter for me if I did. Gave me overnight to think it over."

"That's odd, isn't it?"

"Yes. My wife is in tears. I'm about to lose everything—my freedom, my property, my good name. Everything!"

"What did they mean, 'cooperate'?"

•

"I'll tell you! This was cooked up to pressure me to change my testimony in the divorce! I know what they want. All I have to say is that I am not really sure who I saw that night in Amos Burch's office. That's all!"

"They specifically asked that?"

"No, they never mentioned it. They didn't even hint at it. The only word they used was 'cooperate.' And that could mean anything. But it's true."

Lytell sighed. "Phantasms. Mark St. John is an ethical lawyer, one of the best I've known. He simply would not stoop to obstructing justice or suborning perjury. It's just not in him. And even if it were in him, he wouldn't risk being disbarred and prosecuted himself. And here you are, telling me that his use of the word 'cooperate' is filled with hidden meaning, that this is all a scheme to rescind or correct or modify your testimony in a minor divorce case."

"Yes, sir. That is what I'm saying. But it's not a minor divorce case."

"What will you be charged with?"

"Criminal grand theft. And a civil suit."

"I repeat: how do you know this has anything to do with Mrs. Burch's divorce?"

"I don't. They didn't say a word. They were very careful. But even if they didn't say a word, it's obvious. If I weaken my testimony in the slightest, Boardman will throw it out the window and you'll lose the case. That's what this is about."

Lytell glared. "Do you really believe Amos Burch,

whatever his peccadilloes may be, would resort to this monstrous fraud just to hide an adultery? Subornation of perjury, ruin of an innocent man, seizure of assets that don't belong to him? Really, Daniel, I'm finding this incredible. Burch is a vain man, but would even a vain man do this just to win a divorce case?"

"Yes! If the ground is adultery!"

Lytell studied his new client skeptically. "What else has gone on that you haven't told me?"

"I've told you everything."

"Did you blackmail Amos Burch after seeing the two of them? Is that how you rose so suddenly to the top? How you got yourself a fat raise?"

Daniel stared, speechless, at Lytell.

"Well?"

"I have never varied from the truth. There is nothing to add to what I've told you, and nothing to subtract from it."

"So your story is that Amos Burch is doing all this very serious criminal conduct to get you to alter your testimony." He shook his head. "Not Burch. Fraud and injustice and utterly unethical conduct? Never. Burch is a good and decent man who succumbed to certain temptations that afflict many of us in our lifetimes. Your story doesn't make sense, and frankly, it offends me. My star witness! Do you know what this does to your credibility? You've cost Myrtle her divorce."

Knott saw how this was going. "Yes, that's it. I've

cost Myrtle her divorce. Don't you see? If I need help, will you represent me?"

"I'll think about it. My duty is to Mrs. Burch. If you are convicted as a felon, that'll impeach your testimony and raise the possibility of all sorts of other motives. Who are you, Knott? What's your game?"

"If my testimony is crucial to your case, I'd think you'd defend me."

"I'll make no decision now. This stinks. I want to see what you're charged with, what the evidence looks like, whether there would be a conflict of interest . . . and whether you could pay me."

"I have money in the bank."

"The moment a replevin's filed, you may not. There'll be a lis pendens, which means your property will come under court supervision and you'll be unable to pay a dime until the case is settled."

"What would I do for a lawyer?"

Lytell shrugged. "If you have no assets, the court could appoint one. This county does it by rotation: Streeter, St. John, Lytell in order. But you have assets. You'd probably employ a Durango attorney."

"What should I do, Mr. Lytell? You're my only help."

"Don't run."

"That's it?"

"That's the only certain advice I can give you now. If you're guilty, confess it. Get this stinking thing off the docket."

Knott felt his spirits slide. "You don't believe me."

"I've never said that, Knott. Now, if you'll excuse me—"

Knott stepped into a bitter wind. He realized he hadn't had lunch, but he wasn't hungry. He trudged slowly toward the bank, fighting his impulse to go somewhere, anywhere other than his office, where perfidy surrounded him. But he made himself walk, standing upright. He had done no wrong, and even though it was small comfort in such a time, it remained a comfort still.

He believed in an ultimate justice, not necessarily one that was fulfilled on earth. There were some who would find justice awaiting them only upon their death.

They were waiting for him in his office: St. John and Sheriff Kennear, a man he had often conversed with at the teller's window.

"Sorry, Knott. I'll have to take you in. The bank's discovered wrongdoing, and it points to you," he said. "Pretty fancy stuff, it seems. Now, you can walk in front of me quietly, or I can put manacles on you. A fella like you, you'll walk nice and easy, eh?"

Knott felt himself tumbling, falling, flying through space, as if pushed over a precipice.

He stared into the inscrutable face of Mark St. John. "I have never taken a dime," he said.

"That's right. Never a dime, but more than nine thousand United States dollars," St. John said.

In a way, Kennear was being kind. He let Knott bundle himself in his overcoat—after checking its pockets—and then walk before him, unfettered and without making a public scene. It occurred to Knott that it was an act of contempt. A more dangerous man would have been led away at gunpoint.

But there were all sorts of dangerous men, and Knott realized that maybe he was the most dangerous of all men, the only one who truly threatened Amos Burch's Paradise.

He straightened himself, fighting to stand up under the crushing burden on his shoulders, and walked slowly toward the courthouse and its iron-barred, dark, cold jail.

Chapter 19

Daniel Knott pleaded not guilty at the arraignment. Judge Boardman set bail at a thousand dollars and told the prisoner that he was entitled to a lawyer.

"Everything I possess is tied up by the civil suit. I have no way of making bail and no way to pay a lawyer," Knott said.

"Then you have a problem. I will take the matter under advisement," the judge said. "Your assets are under the supervision of this court."

Knott didn't like the tone of the man presiding behind that raised bench. It all served to remind him that this was Amos Burch's courthouse, as well as Amos Burch's town. Boardman was Burch's handpicked candidate for the office.

"Do you want a lawyer?" Knott saw that the judge had a red-veined nose that suggested an intimacy with spiritous drink.

"Yes."

"I'll appoint Eben Lytell. He's not a bank director and is not employed by Amos Burch, and therefore he can serve."

"He turned me down. I'd prefer an attorney from Durango."

"I've appointed Lytell."

There was a finality about his words. Knott remained silent. There was nothing to say to these people. He felt like a rabbit in the claws of an eagle.

"Docket's almost empty. I'll set a trial date for early January." Boardman peered over his rimless spectacles. "That suit you?"

Knott nodded.

"You will answer yes or no, Knott. The recorder can't report a nod."

"Yes," Knott said. His rising temper was pushing him to say much more, but he clamped his mouth shut.

So his attorney was to be Myrtle Burch's attorney, a man who had refused him and considered his defense outlandish, and the ruin of Myrtle's case.

The sheriff led Knott back to the dark jail cell and herded him inside.

"I would like you to tell my wife I'm here," he said.

Kennear just smiled. Knott wondered if that was a yes or a no, or if the lawman was just being spiteful in his silence.

The gray-enameled door clanged, and suddenly Knott felt a helplessness such as he had never experienced in his life. He could not walk away. He studied the ten-foot-square confines of his cell, seeing a hard bunk with a one-inch thick excuse for a mattress, a slop pail, and a brown blanket. No pillow. The stone walls exuded coldness, and reeked of vomit. This cell was going to suck his life's heat right out of him.

From now on his meals, indeed his very life, depended on others. His contact with his wife and family depended on his jailers. He was going to have much too much time. How did one spend minutes and hours and days in such a place? If he needed a doctor, who would come? If he went mad, who would care? If he died, who would find out?

A single high window bled in some miserly light, scarcely enough to read by, even at midday.

Who would help him? Who would get him out on bail? Who could truly make his case before Judge Boardman and a jury?

He peered about, able to see several other cells in the jailhouse. They were empty. Paradise had little crime, thanks to an efficient law enforcement system and Amos Burch's way of shaping the town to his standards. Knott would neither have fellow prisoners to talk to nor jailhouse lawyers to share ideas with, giving and receiving support. He was alone, incredibly and hopelessly alone.

So Lytell believed his star witness was an embezzler and Knott's testimony would be thrown out. He would do a perfunctory job, and soon enough Knott would find himself being transported by stagecoach and railroad to the penitentiary.

Daniel sat down on the bunk and pulled the thin blanket around him. Was there no heat at all in this jailhouse? Would they at least let him have a sweater or coat?

He knew his first task was discipline; he needed to overcome the sheer desperation that flooded through him. He had to contain his impulse to rattle the iron cage until it fell apart, to drive his fists through stone walls, to twist and bend metal bars until he could walk through them, to kick the concrete floor into rubble, to shoulder the cast-iron ceiling aside, to howl until no one in that sheriff's office could stand it.

He sat on his bunk and forced himself to cool down. That was when the temptation slithered through his heart once again. He could walk away. There might well be good reason why Eben Lytell had, by some process, become the counselor representing one Daniel Knott, bank executive, accused of grand theft and facing years of eternal, indelible shame. It was almost as if this too had been masterminded by Amos C. Burch, the man who didn't want the world to know or believe that he had committed adultery.

He couldn't bear to sit, so he paced. He metered his cell in steps. Three strides by two strides by three strides, round and round, back and forth, solid walls on three sides, gray steel bars and a locked door to freedom on the fourth. He walked until he couldn't anymore, then dropped onto the bunk and stared at nothing. Was this life? Had he come to this because he would not alter a bit of sworn testimony? Was he mad?

Then Lytell arrived, accompanied by a keep who let the lawyer into the cell. Knott stared at the man from his bunk, and only reluctantly sat up.

"Seems I'm your lawyer, Knott," the attorney said, extending a hand.

Knott hesitated, and then shook it.

"I came as fast as I could."

"What time is it?"

"Eleven, little after."

Knott was stunned. Had he been in this cell less than an hour? It seemed like half a lifetime!

"All I have to tell you I can do in two minutes," Knott said. "First of all, I did not do this embezzling; I've never stolen a cent. Once when the books just wouldn't balance, I put some of my own money in because I was so worried about it. It is not even in me to steal from anyone. Those ledger accounts are in my hand, and I started them based on the provisions of each contract. That's all I know."

"No possibility of a mistake?"

"None."

"Well, we'll need to come up with a defense. But my first thought was bailing you out of here. I've talked to a bail bondsman and he'll want two hundred. I've talked with Boardman, and he's releasing that much from your Merchant Bank account, as well as a retainer for me. I'll have you out in a few minutes. You'll be confined to the county, and if you jump bail you'll be in even worse trouble. Once you're out, we'll talk about your case. I don't know what sort of defense you have; it's pretty open-and-shut, but we'll get to that."

"You mean I'll be getting out?"

"Until your trial."

Knott choked back emotion.

"What else did you want to tell me, Knott?"

"That my testimony was as accurate as I could make it, that I have no doubts, and that my testimony's going to stay that way."

Lytell shook his head and then smiled. "What has that to do with this?"

Knott didn't reply. So Lytell was going to play the game too, seeing the embezzlement business as unrelated to the divorce testimony.

"You didn't answer my question."

"I'll answer by asking you one: if I were to amend my testimony, and say I wasn't sure who I saw in an intimate embrace in Amos Burch's office that night, would it change anything?"

Lytell smiled slowly. "That's for you to decide. I personally think it's nonsense. The two aren't related. Amos Burch is simply protecting his bank and his borrowers from theft."

"And is that what you believe?"

Lytell nodded.

"And you think there was a theft?"

"The evidence is compelling, but perhaps we'll find a way to build a case. That's what we'll talk about. And if you don't have much of a case, there is still much I can do. You have a spotless past, you're an able employee, and all that."

"But you think I'm guilty." It wasn't a question.

"We'll look at the charge and see. We'll go over your story, scrutinize every detail you bring up. We'll examine this embezzlement charge from top to bottom. You'll tell me the way the bank keeps its books. You'll tell me why you didn't do it.

"You'll be talking to a skeptic but not a mind that's slammed shut on you. You're going to have to explain why Amos Burch would defy everything he believes in, knowingly hurt you and obstruct justice, just to keep the world from hearing about his little peccadillo. You figure you can persuade me? I've seen a lot of crazy cases in my day, so I'll listen. But we're not talking about some lunatic. We're talking about the honorable Amos C. Burch. And if your story doesn't wash, I want you to know I am still very capable of helping you, if you cooperate."

"That's exactly what Burch's lawyer said—if I cooperate it will go better for me. What case are you referring to?"

Lytell stared. "It is not helpful to have a client who resists counsel."

That was where it stood when Sheriff Kennear appeared, with a clanging of jailhouse doors.

"Got a writ. Okay, Knott. You sign these and you're out on bail. You're in luck to have counsel like this gent."

Knott was so glad to see the open door that he didn't argue.

"Yes, I am," he said gravely.

At least Lytell had given him a few days or weeks of liberty. Time to get his affairs in order. Time to try to defend himself. It was scarcely noon, but he felt he had gone three days without sleep.

The sheriff led him into the office, followed by Lytell, and introduced him to the bail bondsman, someone named Homer Joffe, who presented yet another long agreement, loaded with boilerplate. Then Daniel was allowed to go through the foyer and out into sunlight.

The light was incredible. Sunlight poured down on Paradise setting every building aglow. It flooded into the dark corners of Daniel Knott's soul.

"Get some lunch and then come to my office, Knott," Lytell said.

Daniel Knott turned unsteadily and walked home along stately tree-lined boulevards, past trim homes, to his own house, where Hannah was waiting.

Chapter 20

Hannah was rinsing milk bottles she intended to return to Beck's Creamery that afternoon when she beheld Daniel at the door.

"Oh!" she cried and ran to him.

He hugged her listlessly, and she wondered what was wrong. She drew back and studied him, discovering shocking things in his face—a haggardness she had never seen in her husband.

He steered her into the quiet kitchen, where she had a hen stewing on the wood range.

"They arrested me this morning," he said. Slowly, he described the morning's ordeal, not sparing her the grim realities of life in a cell behind a locked door.

She sat numbly in the bentwood chair, learning about the arraignment, Daniel's innocent plea, the court-appointed lawyer, the judge freeing some funds from Daniel's account, and the bondsman.

How little she understood of such things. That was for other sorts of people.

"I thought I didn't have access to any money, but that's not the way it is," he said. "Lytell explained it during all that bail bond business. Prescott Board-man can allow reasonable expenses. He allowed bail money, and he'll allow us funds to live on, at least until the verdict. This lis pendens writ, or whatever it's called, is just to keep us from hiding assets. It's a good thing we saved some of that bank salary."

It still didn't make much sense to Hannah. This was a world so alien from her domestic one that she could scarcely fathom it.

"Oh, Dan, I'm so glad you're out. Are you hungry?"

Daniel shook his head. He slumped onto the bat-tered old table, resting heavily on his elbows, his face buried in his hands.

"I despise Amos Burch," she said.

"I wish I could just talk to him. He's at the bottom of this. I don't think even his lawyers know what all this is about. Certainly not Eben Lytell. He thinks the embezzlement charge has nothing to do with the divorce."

"Maybe he's right, Daniel. Maybe it's all a mis-take."

Her husband shook his head.

"How do you know?" she asked.

"I just do. I have to go back to Lytell's office and try to explain it. And I can't. Attacking Amos Burch, or suggesting that he's trying to undermine Colorado justice, is like attacking a saint. Lytell isn't going to buy it."

She ached to feed him. She had never seen him turn away from food. She pulled a loaf of her fresh-baked bread from the safe, found some creamery butter in the ice chest, and sliced some bread for him. He stared listlessly but then buttered a piece and nibbled on it, unaware that he was eating anything at all. She set some milk before him, but he just stared at it.

"What are we going to do now, Daniel?"

"I don't know. I've never felt so—so helpless. I have no idea what to do. I don't know from hour to hour. And it's going to get worse. Tomorrow the *Tattler* comes out. I guess you know how it'll look to the neighbors, to everyone in town. The teachers at school. The children. I'm not sure you'll be able to buy meat tomorrow."

"The children?"

He stared miserably at her. " 'Your daddy's a thief!' they'll say. And you, Hannah. Tomorrow people won't greet you. You'll get averted eyes. A lame excuse. The rude request to see your money first. Tomorrow, everything about Paradise'll be mean."

"I will endure. Don't fret about me."

Tomorrow it would start. Isolation. Ostracism. Rudeness. Assumption of guilt. That hurt most. They would assume that Daniel had done what he was accused of doing. That Amos Burch could do no wrong. Maybe they would think that she had a hand in it. She knew intuitively that she could make no argument, or dissuade a single soul in Paradise, where Amos Burch was a demigod, and the Merchant Bank was bulked like a fortress.

If the children ran into real cruelty, she knew she would do something rash. She would not permit it. If things got too bad, she'd pluck them out of Paradise. Her parents lived in Denver, and she might take the children there and hope that the news wouldn't follow them. All of this angered her. How could this happen in the United States of America? How could Daniel escape an unjust prosecution?

Or *was* it unjust? Hastily, she drove that terrible thought out of her mind. It wasn't in Daniel to do it. She knew him so well. Or did she? She hated these perverse little tendrils of doubt, but she couldn't stop them from creeping through her mind.

Daniel rose painfully, donned his greatcoat, kissed her absently—she knew his mind was a thousand miles away—and left her in her warm kitchen, her fortress against a cold world.

He would be going to the office of his lawyer to try to persuade the man of his innocence. The very thought of her quiet, determined husband trying to clear himself to a court-appointed lawyer sent despair through her. Daniel was a simple man, with simple ideas of right and wrong. That was the key to understanding him. If something was wrong, he wouldn't do it.

Eben Lytell wasn't a simple man, and he would regard Daniel as a subtle liar or scoundrel. But

Lytell would be wrong. The thing she loved about Daniel was his simplicity. He just wasn't like most people. He didn't know how to cover up anything, or how to gloss over awkward moments, and that sometimes bothered others. But she loved his simplicity. That honesty was inviting. She had never doubted him. She had never questioned him . . . until now.

She wanted desperately to shield her children. They would come home from school soon, and perhaps she could arm them, warn them, bolster them against the cruelties that would surely afflict them in a day or two. But she scarcely knew what to say.

She drew her cape over her, settled a bonnet on her wavy hair, loaded the milk bottles into a basket, and set out upon the day. She left the bottles at Beck's and picked up two fresh quarts and a pint of cream, then hiked to the post office for the mail. The post office occupied a corner of Rand's Mercantile, and was presided over by an odd character named Horatio Bates, who knew everything about everyone and would soon learn more about the Knott family than it cared to make known.

"Ah, Mrs. Knott," he said from behind his wicket. "I believe there's a letter or two."

He spoke with a certain cultivation not often heard, even among the elite of Paradise. She had always been fascinated by him: an odd duck, with a bald head, massive brow, piercing gray eyes topped by massive lashes, and a rampant curiosity. Some would have called it nosiness. Bates was not shy about probing, either, using postcards and return addresses on his envelopes as levers to worm things out of people.

Triumphantly, he plucked some letters from their pigeonhole and handed them to her.

"And how is Mr. Knott doing?"

"Fine," she said guardedly.

"How did his testimony go?"

"Testimony?"

"In the Burch divorce."

She itched to lie, to deny it all, but she didn't. "I couldn't really say," she said. "I wasn't there."

"Streeter couldn't budge him an inch, I hear."

"Why do you say that?"

"Lawyers, clerks, bailiffs, and lawmen trade news in post offices."

He smiled broadly, his remarkable assessing eyes focusing on her. It was not an unfriendly or judgmental gaze, and she never let his curiosity bother her.

"Daniel would not tell a lie to save his life," she said.

"Is that so?"

She sighed. "Good day, Mr. Bates."

"Wait, Mrs. Knott. I hear things, you know. People come here and visit with each other, oblivious to the old postmaster just on the other side of the counter. It's perfectly astonishing."

"Yes, well, I must be—"

"Why, it's certainly a peaceful afternoon. Now tell

me something. Is it true that some accounts at the bank don't add up?"

"Mr. Bates—"

"I heard it. I thought you might know."

She turned angrily and left. How insidious gossip was! How swiftly it would stab at Daniel, hurting her, bringing her children to tears.

On the boardwalk she examined the letters. One was a monthly statement from Frohmeier's Ice and Coal, another a letter from her mother in Denver, and the third a letter for Rosalie from a pen pal in Durango. No wonder postmasters knew so much. Private lives, with all their secrets, flowed through the pigeonholes of every post office in the country. And a man like Bates made entertainment out of it.

She stopped at Schmidt's Butcher Shop for some pot roast and some soup bones, spending a little of her nest egg, and then she hiked home. Bates had disturbed her. She had hoped for some privacy, some time, but the gossip was flying already, and that Mr. Bates was probably spreading it as fast as he got it. Still, she liked him. Something unique in him fascinated her. It was as if he were looking for the good in people, not the bad. Hadn't he complimented Daniel for testifying as honestly as he knew how?

But when she got home she slid into melancholia. This house, and those within it, were threatened by the coming storm and fire. In early January everything she knew and loved in Paradise might be taken from her. And Daniel might vanish into a cold cruel prison for so long that she might never see him again.

She could not fight the tears, and after jamming the milk and meat into her ice chest, she fled to the bedroom, and no longer tried to stem the tide.

Chapter 21

Knott found Eben Lytell awaiting him in his parlor office, sitting behind that battered desk.

"Well, Daniel, you'd better start at the beginning and tell me your story. You have my assurance that I'll do everything I can. I know how you must feel."

Heartened by even that modicum of sympathy, Knott told his story once again.

Lytell steepled his hands, nodding throughout Daniel's narrative. But when he had finished, Lytell shook his head. "You're asking me to believe the wildest story I've ever heard. Even if I do, the world won't believe that Amos Burch would suborn perjury."

Lytell was so vehement that Knott suddenly believed him. Those lawyers were being duped. No one but Amos Burch was responsible for what was happening to him.

"Mr. Lytell, it's a bluff. I think he'll drop these

charges when he sees I won't budge. He just wanted to push me into saying I didn't see what I plainly saw."

Lytell was incredulous. "Good God, Daniel! Why on earth would a man of Burch's repute and integrity risk it? Especially for a miserable divorce case? Yes, adultery's embarrassing, but it isn't as if he did anything worse than thousands of other husbands."

"For him it's that important. I think it mortifies him some way or another. Being caught in a little embarrassment like Henry Ward Beecher. Remember him? The Congregational minister, lecturer, leader of men, antislavery proponent, suffrage advocate, scientist, New York City saint? Don't you remember?"

"Daniel, if I may say so, your story won't work in court. Do you realize how preposterous it is? How bizarre and far-fetched? Is this really what you want to tell the judge and jury?"

Knott nodded.

"Well, we can check your case out in a hurry. I'm going to look at the evidence that Amos says he has. If need be, I'll look at the mortgage contracts. You can probably give me the names of a dozen people who have loans or mortgages. If their contracts have lower interest rates than you recorded in the ledgers, there isn't much I can do to help you."

"They let me look at a couple. Both of them looked too new to me. Those contracts get pulled out of files and returned several times a year."

"So you're still sticking to the idea that Burch is pressuring you? Why would he do it that way? I can scarcely think of anything more risky."

"Because he doesn't know me, sir. He thought I'd cave in. I'm just an underling, as far as he's concerned. He points a finger and I'm a vice president. He points again and I'm in jail. He never imagined I'd resist, or that he'd have to file a complaint and see it all in court."

"No, Knott, that's not the Amos Burch everyone in this community knows. Give me something else to go on."

"That's all I have, Mr. Lytell."

"You have some grievance against the bank?"

"None."

"Or Burch?"

"Not until this."

"Do you realize what Erich Braunfels is going to do to this story? Do you want to be put on the stand?"

"Yes, I'll tell this to the jury."

"I'd advise against it. We can make a more plausible case that these accounting errors were simply mistakes."

"I did not set up dummy accounts!"

Lytell stared. "We don't seem to be getting anywhere. You're tying my hands. No innocent mistakes. No errors. Just a very strange story about Amos Burch attempting to pressure a witness by highly illegal means. And I suppose you'll want me to say that the firm of St. John and Streeter was all mixed up in it."

"No, sir. I don't think they are. I think Amos Burch cooked this up by himself. I think he didn't want anyone to know or even suspect it."

"So Amos Burch is the criminal, embezzling from his own bank. Is that it?"

"No, sir. I don't think a penny is missing. I think it's a bluff. Burch is pressuring me. But he never dreamed it'd go this far. I think he's worried that he'll be caught."

"Well, God help you if that's what we're presenting to Prescott Boardman's court. You have no evidence! That's quite a story, and you'll have to persuade twelve veniremen that it's true."

His gaze pierced Knott. "Do this: examine the books and make your case for me. We'll have access to the bank ledgers—under supervision, of course. Show me why it's a bluff and show me how Amos Burch set it up. Persuade *me*."

Knott had the sinking feeling that he was being dismissed. Ten minutes later, the interview was over. The only thing Knott got out of it was a sense that Burch's own attorneys had no knowledge at all of what Burch was doing because he had said nothing at all to them.

By the time Daniel reached the street, fear overtook him. Was there no way out? Paradise was seductive that afternoon, the December zephyrs mild, the sun benevolent. Christmas was approaching, and Knott discovered paper ornaments in the shop windows. He had scarcely thought about Christmas. He needed to buy some gifts for Hannah and his children. But with what?

Paradise had changed, and he had no sense of belonging there now. He wished he could sell his home, pack his belongings in crates and casks, ship them to someplace beyond the horizon and far from Colorado, and herd his family aboard one of the lacquered Concord Stages, operated by the San Juan and Durango Coach Line, and into a new and sweeter life.

But he had no choices, and so he would fight, and he would never surrender or sell out. If the price of honest testimony was years in a penitentiary, then that was how his life would spin out.

He headed for the bank, stalked past the gawking tellers and into his old office, now occupied again by Amos Burch, who seemed to fill the room in a way that Knott never could.

Burch looked up, startled.

"What are you doing here?"

"We're going to talk, and I'm going to look at contracts and ledgers."

"You've already looked at them. We gave you that time. Now, if you'll excuse me—"

Knott shut the door.

"Do I have to make myself plainer? Get out. You've robbed the Merchant Bank and I'll not tolerate your presence. Must I summon help?"

"You'll sit there and listen," Knott said, his anger boiling over. "You and I both know something the rest of Paradise doesn't know, and that's that I haven't taken a penny. You and I know that you cooked this up as a bluff. You thought I'd cave in, but I didn't. You didn't expect Dan Knott to stand like a man and hold his ground, and now you're busy trying to make the bluff real enough to pass in court. And you hate it. I testified honestly. I won't change my testimony, and I won't lie just to save you embarrassment."

"Now are you done? Get out."

"I'm not done. The thing is, you can hardly stand this. Destroying me, tormenting my family, robbing me of my reputation and livelihood, reducing my wife and children to rags. You hate it, sending me off to jail for something I didn't do, something you conjured up to save your skin. You know what? You're going to suffer bad conscience for the rest of your life. Every hour of every day, until you meet your Maker, and then you'll suffer all the more. Everything you believed about yourself is a lie."

Burch suddenly smiled. "How you do carry on, Daniel! If you think all of that is true, why, go ahead and prove it. The jury will be all ears."

"Show me the ledgers and contracts. Not the ones you rewrote to put me in trouble, but the originals, with the terms that I copied faithfully. Go ahead, get them and let me see them. They're around some-where."

At last, Knott saw caution and hesitation shroud the powerful visage of Amos C. Burch.

"I will arrange for your attorney to examine the evidence in a week or so. Right now, I'm busy."

"Busy manufacturing a fraud."

Burch rose up like a grizzly bear, and astonishingly, gripped a small-caliber revolver in his gnarled right hand. Its black bore pointed straight at Knott, whose pulse raced at the sight of the loaded weapon aimed at his chest.

"Get out right now. Or I will be forced to shoot you in self-defense."

"All right. I won, didn't I? Your response is to draw a weapon, not to show that I'm wrong. I won, Amos!"

"Out!"

For the smallest moment, the look in Burch's crumpled face told Knott he was right.

He opened the massive door and closed it behind him. The bore of the revolver never wavered, but Burch's eyes radiated a hatred so violent, so electric, that it startled Knott. He was suddenly glad to escape alive.

He strode past the staring tellers, not even acknowledging them, and into the sunlight. Suddenly the sunlight seemed clean, compared to the foulness inside the bank. But his rising spirits were dashed by the newsboy on the corner, Jackie Gabriel, the son of his neighbors.

"Read all about it, bank robbed!" the kid yelled.

"The bank wasn't robbed," Knott snapped.

"Hey! It's you, the crook!"

Knott grabbed a copy of the *Paradise Tattler* and

beheld his own image and a headline that read BANK
EXECUTIVE INDICTED FOR GRAND LARCENY. Slowly he
returned the paper to Jackie, the rest of it unread. He
had no stomach for reading lies in Amos Burch's biweekly rag.

He wondered how his wife and children would
ever get through this terrible day—and the next,
and the next.

Chapter 22

In only a few hours, Hannah Knott's world fell apart. The story of villainy trumpeted by the *Tattler* found its way quickly into every cranny of Paradise.

When she tucked her basket under her arm and went for groceries that December afternoon, neighbors who usually greeted her averted their eyes and hurried past, their lips compressed. And when she entered Malcolm's General Store, Harry Fosdick, the old clerk who always wore the green eyeshade, pursed his lips.

"You got cash?" he asked.

"Put it on our monthly bill."

"No, I ain't doin' that no more. And here's your balance, payable right now or Malcolm says you don't buy a thing."

Indignation boiled up in her. "You seem to think

Daniel's already guilty! Why, there hasn't even been a trial yet!"

He squinted at her from rheumy eyes. "Anybody steals from the likes of Amos Burch should be tarred and feathered and run out of Paradise."

"But he didn't!"

"Paper says the bank made the complaint. Suing to recover assets too. That's enough for me. Treating Amos Burch that way."

"When this trial's over and Daniel's free, we'll take our trade elsewhere." She glared at him.

"He'll be off to the pen, and you just go ahead and spend your pile of stolen money somewhere else. That's what I say, and old Malcolm, he thinks twice as hard on it as me because he's the owner."

She dug into the solitary coins in her pocket. "I need a pound of oatmeal," she said, thrusting a four-bit piece at him.

"Your money ain't good enough here."

"I have children to feed!"

"Shoulda thought of that before you began lifting cash outa the bank's till."

She fumed. "Are you judge and jury? Have you heard the evidence?"

"The word of Amos Burch is all the evidence I'll ever need in this lifetime."

"But how am I going to feed my family?"

He grinned. "I reckon they ought to starve right smartly."

"You have such Christian charity!"

"I'd rather feed alley cats than a peck of Knotts."

Two women approached the counter, paused suddenly, whispered to each other, and drew themselves up starchily.

"We can't avoid you, but we don't wish to greet you," said one.

Hannah saw how this was going, and she nodded curtly and headed for the double doors.

She stepped out into the windy street. Winter was blowing off the San Juan peaks, and she shivered in its icy grasp. She stood numbly, scarcely able to think, and finally turned toward the Merchant Bank a block away. Walking toward that building was like stepping into the fangs of a rattlesnake, but she had to do it.

She entered the quiet confines of the bank and let its warmth permeate her cloth coat and touch her cheeks. It was a gracious place, and she gazed up at the high ceiling of pressed metal, the shining floors of polished and textured concrete, the brass fittings around the teller windows, and the dark paneling.

She approached the window manned by her old friend Jasper Pickering.

He stared at her, stiff-lipped.

"I wish to withdraw twenty dollars from my savings," she said.

His Adam's apple bobbed twice. "I can't do that, Mizz Knott."

"It's my money."

"Can't do it."

"It's mine, not anyone else's!" She had opened the savings account soon after they arrived in Paradise and had slipped her dimes and pennies into it for years. Now it totaled ninety-seven dollars.

"Court order—sorry, Mizz Knott."

"I must speak to Amos Burch!"

He looked acutely embarrassed and was obviously relieved when she stepped away.

She found Burch in his usual haunt and entered without knocking.

"I wish to withdraw money from my own personal savings," she said.

He looked up, pushing aside the scowl that settled fleetingly on his face, and smiled cheerfully. "How fine to see a great lady," he said. "The fairest of the fair. Now, what can I do for you?"

"My children need to be fed, and so do I. I wish to use my own funds to do so."

He sighed, unhappily, and stared at some point just above her bonnet. "My hands are tied by the court, you know."

"But it's my own money!"

"Well, you see, there's some question about that. Maybe you bear some complicity in all this sad business. Maybe some of poor Daniel's loot was stashed in your little account. A wife's account is so handy to hide things in."

She dug into her reticule and extracted a savings passbook.

"Here! Pennies and dimes, that's all it ever was!"

He sighed. "How I wish I could help you. But I'm putty in the hands of my lawyers. It's not for my sake, but for the sake of the bank's customers. Our integrity is at stake here."

She fought back tears.

"I'll help," he said, extracting a silver dollar from his trousers. "I abhor suffering."

She stared at it, that dollar lying in his soft white hand, and at him, gazing blandly upon her.

"You cannot buy me, or Daniel, with one piece or thirty pieces of silver," she said.

He smiled and slipped the dollar into his pocket. "Just charity. Too bad about Daniel," he said.

She fled that suffocating office, traced her way down the hall past the staring tellers, and out the doors. The winter air felt clean, sharp and fresh, and did not have the aroma of evil as did Burch's office.

She trudged to the south end of town, found the hostler at the livery barn, and bought a gallon of rolled oats, which he poured into a flour sack. After she paid the man two bits, she hiked home. Her children would have oatmeal one way or another, and the hostler didn't know who she was—or maybe didn't care.

She walked into the wind going home, and it pierced every cranny of her clothing straight to her skin. But she ignored it. Her mind was on other things. Her poor Daniel. She admired him, loved him dearly. She wished he could bend a little. She felt confused, because his honor was one of the things she adored in him. His honor made her feel secure in his company and in his arms. He was a good man. But his rectitude was inflicting unbearable things upon her.

The children were home.

Peter and Daniel Junior were hiding in their room. Rosalie, poor thing, slumped at the kitchen table, tearstained and wounded.

"Oh, Rosy," she said, setting aside her basket and drawing the girl to her.

"It's not true, it's not true!" the girl cried. "They're so mean!"

"Who? The students?"

"The principal, Mr. Kessler. He told me to go home and not return today."

Hannah marveled. "He did? Did he say why?"

"He just said go home. He made me leave my *McGuffey's Reader*."

"He can't do that. I'll talk to him tomorrow."

Rosalie snuffled and clasped her mother and wouldn't let go.

"I have to see about the boys," Hannah said.

She knocked on the boys' door and got no response.

"It's Mother. I want to talk to you."

Peter mumbled something. She opened the door, seeing the boys on their slender beds. She saw at once that Danny had been in a fight. His lip was swollen, and his face and hands were bruised and dirty.

"Dan, what happened?"

He didn't respond.

"Dan?"

"They threw rocks at him," Peter said. "He called them liars, and they all landed on him and he got into a fight. I tried to pull them off him, and we got away, but they threw rocks."

"Were you hit?"

"Yes."

She sat on Dan's bunk and found his hand, holding it gently.

"Your dad's not a crook. He's the most honest man there is. You just believe that and don't let them taunt you. If they gang up, just walk away. They're just wanting to bait you into fighting so they can hurt you. That's how gangs work. You just walk away and feel proud of yourselves, of us, and of your father. This is all a mistake. We'll just hold our heads up and know what kind of people the Knotts really are. Don't ever feel ashamed, no matter what people say. We've taught you to be just as honest as you know how. That's what your father is. And what I try to be."

But Danny just stared. She knew his spirit was shattered like a dropped tumbler and that he could not sit in his classes and endure the taunts, perhaps from his teacher as well as the other students.

"You just rest," she said. "When your father comes home, he'll talk with you."

She left them alone, closed their door with an aching heart, and set about cooking up a meager meal.

Maybe Daniel found some answers this afternoon. But when he stumbled through the door, one glance told her he had found no answers at all this terrible day.

Chapter 23

As weary as he was, Daniel Knott knew he had to help his sons and daughter. Today their world collapsed, just as his and Hannah's had. A wave of guilt rose in him: it was his unyielding pride that was responsible for this torment that had befallen his family.

They stared furtively at him throughout the supper that Hannah had managed to put on the table. In the gauzy light of the coal-oil lamps, they looked small and vulnerable. They had mumbled their way through grace, toyed with their food, and would not look him in the eye. He wanted them to eat first. Children were calmer and quieter after they had eaten.

But they didn't swallow much. Danny's bruised and swollen lip made it awkward for him to put anything in his mouth. They had all been crying, and not even the mandatory wash before sitting down to table had erased the stains of their torment.

Hannah rose and started to clear the table, but Daniel stayed her with a small gesture. She returned to her seat, solemnly, and waited for him.

"I am sorry this has come to you," he said. "And it's going to get worse. Your friends are going to snub you and call you names and tell you your father is a thief. Even the teachers might treat you badly. And all our neighbors, too. That's because they think I stole money from the bank."

At least they were listening. Danny was pretending not to, wagging his foot, looking ready to bolt.

"We can get through this, and we can be brave. Each of you has the strength and courage to get through it. It is in you to be strong, and all you have to do is know how strong you are, and how little others can hurt you if you remain strong."

He wondered whether his words would help at all. Words didn't have the force of those rocks the boys were throwing at his sons. But words were all he had. Words and prayers and love.

"First of all, I did not steal so much as one cent from the bank. I will swear it before God and man. I will ask you to believe it because it's true, and also because I'm your father and I won't lie to you."

Peter was staring miserably at him, and Knott wondered whether the boy believed a word of it at all.

"These accusations, and this indictment, were not a mistake. They are not based on some error in the accounts or the ledgers. There is a more terrible reason why I have been accused of a serious crime. This is an effort to make me tell a lie in court. It is no mistake. If I were to tell the lie, under oath, then I am quite certain these charges would be dismissed and it would somehow be discovered that I had not stolen anything. This is what is going to be painful to you. I'm not going to change my testimony. I have to tell the truth just because it's the right thing to do. There isn't any other reason. And that means that this pressure on me isn't going to work.

"I'm not going to tell you who is doing this to me, or what the lie is about. You'll learn about those things when you're older. All I can tell you is that I won't dishonor myself by lying and that I am terribly sorry that this is hurting you so much. Have you any questions so far?"

He gazed at each one at a time, seeing furtive shakes of the head, or in Rosalie's case, just a wounded stare.

"If you don't have to hurt us, then don't!" Peter said.

Knott caught his breath. "That very thought tears me to pieces, Peter. I could put a stop to this tomorrow. But I can't. Strange as it seems, I'm not capable of it."

This time it was Hannah whose wounded gaze pierced him.

"If school becomes too much for you, we'll keep you at home and school you here. I don't want you to suffer. Some people are cruel, no matter what age they are.

"Rosalie, Peter, Danny, there's something you can say to anyone who's trying to hurt you: just tell them that in the United States of America, a person's considered innocent until adjudged guilty in a court of law. Just tell them that. Tell them that you expect them to do what's right, which is to wait and see. I think maybe some teachers, or the principal, might think twice if you say that."

"If the court says you hafta go to jail, then what?" Peter sounded truculent.

"We'll do this one day at a time, Peter. I'm going to spend the next few weeks until the trial trying to prove I'm innocent. Now, I know how boys are. They sometimes pick on someone who's odd, or who doesn't fit in, or who their parents object to. They're going to pick on you.

"If they start bothering you after school, you'll want to run, but they'll be faster and catch you and maybe hurt you again. If you can find the courage, don't run. Stand very still and hold your ground. They'll taunt you and try to goad you into a fight so they can all land on you—but don't fight. It is not cowardice to refuse to fight a whole gang.

"Just stand straight, stand proud, because when you stand upright they'll know it and back off. Draw yourself up, lift your chin, and don't give an inch. They'll respect you even if they don't say so. Standing quiet and tall is the bravest thing a young man can do. If you want to say something, just tell them that their words don't hurt you."

Peter might manage it, he thought. But little Danny was too young. Danny would run, be tackled and pounded, and find his way home in tears.

"Put on your coats, and we'll step outside and I'll show you what truth is like," he said.

He stood, and they did too, suddenly curious. Hannah helped Rosalie bundle up against the Christmas chill. Then Knott led his children into the icy night, into their yard. Overhead, the black sky bristled with pinpoints of light.

"Now, we're going to look at the stars," he said. "Just as we did before. There's the Big Dipper and the North Star. And turn this way and you can see Orion, with his belt and sword. He comes only in the winter, and then slips below the southern horizon. Orion comes and goes, like many men. He brings the sword and then goes away, just like soldiers.

"But turn now and look at the North Star. See it? It's not very bright, is it? But it's always there. Every moment of every year, it is due north. Even the Dipper revolves around it. See the handle? Next month the Big Dipper will be in a different place.

"Now I want you to think about this. Truth is like the North Star. It's always there. What's true will last forever. What's not true comes and goes, twists and turns. Lies don't last, but truth survives forever. For thousands and thousands of years, before there were people. And for thousands and thousands of years into the future, when we are long gone. That's what truth is, and why God likes truth, and why there is a commandment against bearing false witness.

"So, you just think of me touching the North Star now. Some people call it Polaris. I'm going to swear to you, on the North Star, that I did not steal anything from the bank."

Rosalie found his hand and held it. The boys peered awkwardly toward the ice-dotted heavens, mostly to conceal the terrible emotions churning inside them. "All right, we'll go help your mother clear. Whenever you're treated badly by boys or teachers or neighbors or strangers, you just think of the North Star. All right?"

They filed silently into the swift warmth of the house, and Knott followed. He had armed them as best he could, and perhaps inspired them as well. He had shared a little paternal wisdom with them, all the while wondering whether a father could, alone, resist the massive wrenching of their world by a man obsessed with keeping one small, shameful secret.

Later, after the children had fled to their rooms, Knott turned down the lamps until the parlor was lit only by the glow in the joints of the stove and pulled Hannah down beside him on the stiff sofa.

"Mr. Knott," she said, "you acquitted yourself with honor tonight."

He took her hand. "They scarcely know what's in store for them," he said. "I made no progress today.

My lawyer thinks I'm a liar. Amos Burch is looming like a thunderhead. I'm going to be deemed guilty by any jury in this county."

She didn't reply for a long moment.

"What will happen to us?" she asked in a small voice.

"We'll take it one day at a time."

"The children will carry scars the rest of their lives. Are you so sure you're doing what's right?"

"No, I'm not sure at all. I'm in a room without light, trying to find a way out. Hannah, if I've sounded assured, I don't mean to. The truth is, I'm lost and wandering aimlessly. I feel so helpless I can't even describe the feeling to you. When I see you suffering, and the children, I'm torn to pieces."

"Yes! And if you go to prison, what's left for us? Four lives, those you love most, depend on your every word and deed. Have you thought how it'll be? You in prison, year after year? The four of us starving and unwelcome?"

He hadn't an answer to something like that.

"Couldn't you talk to Mr. Burch and find some way to compromise?"

"Say what isn't true?"

"Just—compromise. Talk to him. Ask him what he wants. Find out. Maybe it would be something you could live with. Daniel, I just can't stand this anymore. I'm a mother, too, you know. Must you do this to our children?"

Knott felt worse then he had ever felt in his life.

Hannah was begging him, pleading, with tears and love, to bend a little.

"Hannah. I love you."

"And you love honor more."

He felt a sadness steal into him that he could not resist.

"I need some time, Hannah. Tomorrow I'm going to try something else."

She didn't say anything. She rose slowly and headed up the steep stair to their room, and he knew she had become as distant from him as the cold North Star, and that his union with her would not survive the winter's onslaught.

Chapter 24

The rap on the door puzzled Eloise Joiner. She was expecting Amos, but not this early. Later they would have a Christmas dinner. He never knocked anyway, so it had to be neighbors, perhaps with some Christmas cookies.

She wiped her hands on her apron and headed through the kitchen and the cold parlor, which echoed hollowly, to the door. She wished she could abandon the ranch and live in Paradise, but Amos wouldn't allow it.

She opened the door to the last person she had expected to see: it was Daniel Knott who stood there, his face reddened by the raw wind.

"You!" she said.

"Mrs. Joiner, may I talk with you?"

"There's nothing I have to say to you, of all people."

"Well, I have things to talk about."

"Why should I say a word to a man who's doing his best to ruin my reputation? And Amos's too?"

"I walked a long way to see you. I'd like five minutes, Mrs. Joiner."

"You walked? Here?"

"I have no money to rent a livery barn horse and buggy."

She surrendered, reluctantly. "Well, be quick about it. I'm expecting company soon."

She led him into the kitchen, where he pulled off his woolen cap and gloves and scarf and opened his heavy coat. He hovered over the range, soaking up its warmth.

She did not invite him to sit, nor did she offer him any of the mince pie cooling on the kitchen table.

"Well, Mr. Knott?"

"You're the only person who can help me."

"Why should I even want to?"

"Well, just because truth is truth, lies are lies, and injustice is injustice."

She wasn't liking this. "Say what you have to say, and be on your way. I'm sorry to be rude, but you are presuming on my patience."

"Have you testified at that divorce trial? Things are so secret I don't know what's happened."

"I was deposed."

"What did you say, if I may ask?"

"I've been told to remain strictly silent about it, Mr. Knott. Mr. Burch warned me, and I'll abide by his request."

"Who deposed you?"

"Mr. Lytell."

"I guess you told him you weren't in town that night, or anything else to discredit me. Was that it?"

"Daniel Knott, it is none of your business."

"It is my business. Because I testified truly, an injustice is being done. I'm facing prison for embezzlement, yet I never took a cent. It's Amos Burch's way of pressuring me to change my testimony about seeing something not meant for my eyes—and I'll not change it. If you want injustice to be done, all you have to do is say nothing. If you want justice, and you believe in it, and believe in truth, and being honest under oath, then maybe you'll go to Mr. Lytell and tell him the truth."

"I've heard enough. Please leave."

"I'd like another minute or two."

She acquiesced, not knowing just why.

"I could lie, and spare myself and my family, my children, my wife. But it'd be better if you just retracted what you said in that deposition—"

"How do you know what I said?"

"Because it would all be over, and Myrtle Burch's divorce would be granted, if your testimony was true. There would be undisputed grounds for divorce. I don't rightly know why you're protecting him. I'd think you'd want Myrtle to get that divorce. Unless that happens, you're going to live out here and hardly ever get to town, living forever with something you feel bad about."

"That's it, Daniel. Please leave now."

He stepped reluctantly away from the range.

"You just think about it. Amos would send me to jail and ruin my reputation just to hide something that no one much cares about."

"He cares deeply. He said that if we're discovered . . . it'd be like an unraveling cloth, the thread pulling our fabric apart until nothing's left."

"And so you lied under oath."

"Out!"

She itched to pound on this stupid man with all his sanctimony and nonsense. He had no idea what it was like to be a widow, in debt, in danger. She pushed him to the parlor door and opened it. "Don't ever come back. Don't ever talk to me again."

"You think about it. I think you're a woman who'd like to do the right thing. Unless you do, you'll have a hand in it."

"In what?"

"Destroying my life. And in the end, destroying your own. If you're like most decent people, your conscience won't let you alone."

She hurried him out onto the porch and into the raw wind. "If you think you impressed me, forget it. You didn't. You're simply a rude man."

He smiled suddenly. "I'm sorry," he said gently. "I think you're a lovely woman in trouble, with a heart and soul of pure gold. You'll do what's right when you think on it."

She slammed the door, mostly so he could not see the explosion of tears that erupted. She hated this. Hated the false testimony that she had given in the deposition, hated the lengthy coaching from Amos in how to dodge and weave and mislead, how to cover every possible question, how to plead a faltering memory. And for what? For the sake of his vanity. So that the world might never know that he had committed one of the Seven Deadly Sins, broken a commandment. For an instant she hated and despised Amos Burch, but then resignation and reality seeped in. She was just as trapped by Amos as Daniel Knott.

From the window she watched him brave the wind, tugging his scarf higher about his neck, and trudging toward Paradise. Along the way he would run into Amos, and that meant trouble. She would tell Amos everything. She would tell exactly what Knott wanted, what he said and what he believed, and Amos would turn quiet and watchful, and she knew her lover would then be at his most dangerous.

Some of what Knott said pierced her very core. If only Amos would simply acquiesce in Myrtle's divorce. If it meant that Amos would be free and could marry Eloise, the embarrassment and shame would be worth it. The world understood and forgave these things. She could not fathom why Amos was so rigid, so willing to destroy a man and his family just for his pride.

She didn't feel like cooking, and she felt even less like Christmas. She pushed pots to the edge of the range, doffed her apron, and settled in the horsehair sofa, upset, angry, guilty, and pensive. Why did

Daniel Knott come and ruin Christmas Eve? She loathed him: naïve, simpleminded, too stupid for his own good. Yet honest. She knew he hadn't taken a cent from the bank. She knew it in her bones, and knew Amos was fully capable of destroying Daniel Knott for the sin of exposing a single, modest flaw in the fabric of Burch's character.

Stupid Dan Knott, making her feel bad, feel as if she were conspiring to wreck a good man's life. It was all an accident. He should never have walked into the bank that summer night. Amos had said they'd be alone. She had come to town to shop—she always did on Fridays, and she always put up her buggy at the livery. But ever since Amos had insinuated himself into her life, rescuing her from poverty, her will was not her own. A good man and a great moral force he might be in Paradise, but the price was his control of every facet of its life. As well as hers. She knew she was just as guilty as he. It had been flattering. And she was lonely. Not that she lacked suitors—half the bachelor ranchers in Archuleta County had found reasons to visit her.

But they were not the same as the smooth, gentle, affectionate Amos Burch. And so it had been her doing as much as his. It had just happened. One moment they were conversing; the next, she was riding the whirlwind.

And here was Daniel Knott in the eye of the storm, walking five miles to appeal to her conscience. Well, damn him, he was right, and it tormented her. He wanted her to rescind her deposition. She had told

Lytell that her relationship with Amos Burch was simply business, which had grown into pleasant friendship. He had helped her by putting his own cattle on her place; he had lent her enough to pay the semiannual mortgage payment. Nothing more. Yes, she was in town that night—Burch wanted her to admit it because the livery barn hostler would know that—but she was at the hotel. That was true in a way. She had taken the precaution of taking a room.

She did not like to lie. The deposition, given to that harsh and relentless Eben Lytell, had frequently reduced her to anguish, and she had had to leave the room and compose herself. There she was, under oath and trying desperately to say exactly what her benefactor wanted her to say. She was poor at it, and every false word shot pain through her.

But she had stuck to her guns, even as Alden Streeter watched with a curious frown. He did little to help her except to fend off the ferocious Lytell from time to time. Little did Burch's own lawyer understand what Amos was compelling her to say and do. How she despised herself for surrendering to his will. It was as if he had magical, godlike powers over her own will and over that of the county.

So her deposition contradicted Knott's testimony. Burch had told her he didn't intend to testify. She knew why: he still fancied himself the soul of rectitude and had no intention of perjuring himself. But he was quite content to let others perform that little task for him.

Just last week, while lying beside her, he had told
her a few things about the carefully sealed trial:
Myrtle's testimony had been powerful. She had
kept track of his comings and goings, had collected
ticket stubs from the pockets of his suits. She had
testified about his indifference to her and his disin-
terest in intimate relations. The hostler had pinned
down not only Eloise Joiner's visits to town but also
most of Burch's travels out to her ranch. Amos kept
his horse and buggy there. Amos had sounded as if
he were ready to throttle that stall-mucking moron,
and in fact, there would soon be a firing.

All of this made a powerful circumstantial case,
capped by Knott's eyewitness testimony, which he
stuck to without exception. And that, he explained,
was why Eloise's deposition was so important. And
why it was necessary to awaken the young man,
Knott, to his own peril.

What made her feel bad was that she was being
unjust to Myrtle, who deserved the divorce and a
large settlement. Suddenly, there in her morris chair,
she found herself despising Amos Burch and wish-
ing he was not, even then, riding in his black buggy,
drawn by his prized El Morocco, toward her ranch
home. What sort of crooked, twisted, rotten Christmas was this?

Chapter 25

Amos C. Burch could scarcely believe the apparition on the valley road. There before him, in the flesh, and looking chilled to the marrow, was Daniel Knott. He was plainly hurrying back to Paradise before the long purple shadows of the afternoon overtook him. Walking home. *After visiting Eloise.*

Burch pulled gently on the lines, bringing the restless El Morocco to a prancing halt. The buggy creaked in the buffeting wind. This was a lonely patch of road, with no ranch in sight, the brooding and bleak San Juans hemming the valley floor. A gloomy place, suitable for the gloomy business about to unfold. Burch wagged his buggy whip comfortably. It made a splendid weapon.

But he had no intention of applying the lead-weighted tassels to Knott. What he wanted was to find out exactly what had transpired. To do so would require diplomacy. He needed to know whether Eloise had betrayed her trust and confided anything to Knott, and that could be wormed out of the young man just by asking. He waited for Knott to draw up, loathing him with every fiber of his being.

"Merry Christmas, Amos," Knott said, as he passed El Morocco.

"What are you doing here?"

Knott seemed almost cheerful, which struck Burch as inane. A man about to be sent up for a dozen years ought not to be cheerful about it. Knott didn't reply.

"I'll tell you what you were doing. You walked out to Eloise Joiner's, looking for some way to bring trouble upon me."

"I don't wish trouble upon you, Amos. I only wish to clear myself of your accusations."

"And what has she to do with it?"

"I think you know."

"She has nothing to do with it, and I will tell you bluntly that if you ever visit her again I'll put the sheriff on you."

Knott replied in a measured cadence. "I think that is for her to say, Amos. It is not illegal to visit people."

"Nonetheless, you heard me, Knott. And don't call me Amos."

"But she has everything to do with it. If she were to amend her deposition while she still can, she would put an end to this. Grounds for divorce would be well established. Myrtle would get the divorce she desires, and you would have no reason to pressure me with false accusations of theft in order to get me to lie."

Burch looked around, seeing only the lonely wastes of the foothills and the deepening shadows. "Your time is running out, Knott. You're within a few days of being sent up to prison. There is still time—if you act now."

"And how might I change my fate?" The young man was staring so intensely that Burch had trouble meeting his gaze.

"I think you know," Burch said.

"No, I don't. Say it."

Burch weighed the matter. This lay at the heart of everything. They were alone. He made a swift decision.

"You only thought you saw me last June. We both agree you didn't. It was dark, and you couldn't be sure. It could have been the swamper. There, that's plain enough . . . it's your sole escape, Knott."

"Well, I'm glad it's on the table between us at last. For weeks you've denied the obvious. How did you alter the books?"

"Enough of that."

"You couldn't very well falsify contracts, not with the borrowers holding a copy, so you forged the ledger accounts. I finally remembered something. Your hand and mine are quite similar. You had only to master a few of my capital letters. No wonder I thought I was seeing my own hand. All you did was copy my ledgers with falsified interest payments and set up a couple of dummy accounts where the proceeds ended up. But in actuality, not a cent left that bank."

"Knott, do you realize what you're saying, and who you're saying it to?"

Knott paused, choosing his words carefully. "I'm saying it to a man who's gone wrong. A man whose vanity overrides his justice and honor. A man who's more concerned about hiding a little lapse than about honor. But a man who might come to his senses and redeem himself."

Burch waved his buggy whip menacingly.

"Buggy whips don't change my mind, Mr. Burch. Force doesn't change truth. I'll stick with the truth. Nothing you do to ruin me will alter that."

"You'll find out what buggy whips do, Knott." Burch felt fury mount in him, and he lashed at Knott, who tried to dodge the whistling whip. The lead-tasseled popper cut cruelly across Knott's cheek. The young man staggered, cried out, and reeled backward. The second blow did no damage, snapping across Knott's thick coat. Knott rolled out of the whip's range and tried to stanch the blood on his cheek with a handkerchief, groaning.

"Take it as a warning," Burch yelled, and cracked the whip over El Morocco. The dray horse lurched forward. Behind him, Knott lay in the frozen ruts of the valley road, writhing in pain. Burch thought it would be a fruitful lesson. But shame clawed at him. How had he come to this? Wasn't he the conscience of his community?

Amos Burch rode out the valley in a haze of fury and mortification. So Eloise had told Knott about the deposition. He wondered what else that perfidious woman had said to Knott.

The man exasperated him. He simply wouldn't break or cave in. Every new turn of the screw seemed only to increase his determination to stand his ground. Burch couldn't bear it. Knott alone, in Paradise, had the courage to resist him, and for that Knott would find his life so destroyed that he would never recover. Knott was as good as dead. When he walked out of prison, he would be a soft, hopeless old hulk. The reality of it desolated Burch. He really didn't want that to happen. It was never intended to happen. But now he couldn't stop it. Things had spun utterly out of control.

The horse trotted through the dusky wilderness, and with each step, shame seeped through Burch. He was a good man, with the highest ideals, a profound spiritual nature, unquestioned charity and generosity. Why had he done this? Why did Daniel Knott drive him berserk? Who was this bank teller, this naïve, rigid young man? And why did he excite such fury in him?

Christmas or not, Eloise was going to hear about this. In spite of all his coaching and warnings, she had obviously sung songs. But as he approached her ranch house and saw the glow of her lamp in the window inviting him in, he relented. She was, after all, his heart's desire, and the dinner she was preparing and the joys that would follow had been on his mind for days. He intended to have a Christmas unlike any he had ever had with Myrtle. In the buggy were certain gifts that would make an alluring woman all the more alluring.

He would set the matter aside. She was on probation.

His splendid horse needed no prompting to stop at the front porch. She awaited him at the door, dressed in her best frock, her face and hair aglow in the warm lamplight, her erect posture and fine jaw and chiseled face the price of his life, the ultimate joy in his empire.

He gathered his gifts, wrapped in tissue and tied with bright bows, and alighted from the buggy, which creaked in the icy wind.

"Ah, my own Eloise," he said, hugging her warmly. "Let me put these inside, and let me put El Morocco in the barn stall and I'll be ready for this blessed occasion."

Minutes later, with his horse enjoying a bait of oats and the buggy in the barn aisle, he returned to the warm glow of the house.

"Open the presents," he said. "They came all the way from Denver."

"Wouldn't you like to have some spirits or eat our dinner first?"

"Aha! We'll save the best for last!"

Wordlessly she took off her apron, sat on the settee and loosened the paper. She lifted off the pasteboard cover and gasped. The ermine-trimmed blue coat had set Amos back a pretty penny, and Eloise knew it. He wanted her to know it. He wanted her to know that he could afford anything her heart desired, and that she had formed an alliance with no less than a man of power and taste and vision.

She pulled the bulky coat from its nest of tissue, and held it up.

"Amos—it's beautiful."

"Put it on."

She did, and of course it fit. He knew every measurement that limned Eloise Joiner. "Amos, thank you. Where would you like me to wear this?"

"Why—"

"In town?"

"Well—"

"I will wear it here," she said, and he detected irony in her tone. To wear it in town would flamboyantly advertise her connection to him. It was not the sort of coat that could be bought from the proceeds of a hardscrabble ranch.

She presented her gift box to him, and in it he discovered something more discreet: an afghan she had been knitting for weeks. It would make him a fine carriage robe or cover him in his office when the wind blew.

She poured some claret from a cut-glass decanter he had given her.

"Mr. Knott was here. You must have seen him on the road," she said.

He had expected to dig that out of her later—she was surprising him.

"Yes, I saw him. What did he want?"

"I expected you would ask that. Mostly to tell me things about himself. He said only I could rescue him from an unjust fate. He wanted me to correct my deposition."

"Oh?"

"He makes a connection between Myrtle's divorce proceedings and his indictment for embezzlement. That surprised me at first."

"Well, that's the thinking of a lunatic or a desperado."

"Well, I think it might be true, Amos."

Her words hung there.

"My God, Eloise, what are you saying?"

"Amos, Daniel Knott doesn't seem the type to steal from the bank. He doesn't seem the type to lie, either. I trust my instincts. Women have instincts that men don't know about. I think you should help him. I like him, even if whatever's left of my reputation lies in tatters. I've decided that it doesn't matter. I'm a fallen woman, so it may as well be known to the world."

Amos wrestled back his rage and smiled blandly. "Forget this, Eloise. Forget that swindler and humbug. He's not worthy of your attention. Come now, let's make merry. Put on the feast and then I'll give you another gift."

She arose silently, pulled her apron over her head and tied it, and when she faced him, her eyes revealed a soul so haunted that he knew his Christmas lay in ruins.

Chapter 26

One look at Daniel as he closed the door behind him, and all the Christmas cheer fled Hannah. She had struggled to make this a memorable feast in spite of the lack of presents and the bare subsistence that Judge Boardman had meted out from the impounded funds.

"Daniel! What happened?"

He spotted Rosalie and Peter within earshot. "We'll talk about it later," he said.

A raw, open slash angled across Daniel's left cheek, narrowly missing his eye. That side of his face had swollen so much that it slurred his speech.

He tugged off his greatcoat and slumped, too weary to wash himself. She pulled cookpots to the edge of her kitchen range, drew some hot water from the stove reservoir, gathered towels and soap, and tugged him upstairs into their room, shutting the door behind them.

"Burch," he said. "Met on the road. He knew where I'd been and didn't like it."

"But what did he do?"

"Oh, I provoked it. I told him a thing or two. And for once, he told me a thing or two. The man peered about, looking for ears, it seemed, before saying a thing. But it's clear: he's pressuring me with this false accusation. He said so . . . he actually said it! I got something done, anyway. I smoked him out of his lair and into the open. He's told me what he hasn't even told his own lawyers—that everything he's done to me was calculated to break my will and make me lie under oath."

She dabbed gently with a hot compress, but he winced every time, no matter how gently she wiped. "Oh, Daniel," she said.

"Clean it up. I don't want it to mortify," he said. "I'll just stand the pain."

"I hate to hurt you."

"Got to clean it," he said. "Maybe it was worth it, getting Burch to admit it. Now I don't have any doubts. This wasn't an accounting error."

She wrestled with his face, appalled at the swelling, at the angry flesh and bluish tints that radiated from the vicious cut.

"Buggy whip," Daniel said. "I blame myself. No one else to blame. I told him he was a forger. I saw the heat rise in him like a volcano ready to blow. I was warned well enough, but I just prodded him into it. This'll hurt for a week, but it was worth it."

"You haven't told me about Mrs. Joiner."

"I got there ahead of Burch by half an hour or so. She was setting up for a dinner. Two places set. I could see what sort of Christmas Eve she'd planned. She didn't much want to talk and asked me to leave. But I kept talking, and I got a little from her even though she said she couldn't say a word, that she was under obligation. But I just kept on pressing and finally she melted a little.

"She'd been deposed by Eben Lytell and said she couldn't talk about it. But I got enough from her to know she'd lied, and that Burch made her do it, even coached her. She was feeling mighty bad about it because she's a pretty decent gal. She's afraid of Burch, afraid of her benefactor. Funny thing is, Hannah, she's someone I like—someone with a big heart and a bigger soul.

"She was sort of taking to me after a bit. I don't think she likes her life right now, out there alone, with Amos Burch's little secret hidden from the people of this town, and no one but herself on a ranch she'd just as soon get shut of."

"It must be awful. But she can only blame herself," Hannah said, dabbing at him fiercely. She totally disapproved of Eloise Joiner.

"I guess she's blaming herself, all right. But somehow—ow, that hurts, dammit—I guess some good came of it. I told her who I am and what happened, and she seemed, well, stricken. I startled something inside her, and maybe it'll help us someday. Someday, after the iron doors shut behind me. At least now she knows where her lying is leading another human being."

Hannah sighed, feeling helpless to do much about either the disfiguring and brutal gash or his despair. "I've tried hard to make this a joyous Christmas," she said, her own desolation welling up. "I have three oranges. One for each. That's all we have to give them, Daniel."

He sagged. "I got so busy trying to fight off this indictment I hardly thought of it. I've nothing for you. I've failed my family once again."

She didn't assure him he hadn't, because that very thought bored through her heart over and over, a small sour invasion of what had once been a good marriage. He could still stop this. He could bend a little. Now Christmas, what little there would be of it anyway, lay in ruins.

"I'll lie down until you put the meal on," he said. "I—I've got a headache."

She squeezed his hand, picked up the bloody towel and bowl, and left him. There wasn't any more she could do.

She struggled with the contradictions clamoring for her attention. She knew she should esteem him for his rare honesty and courage, his fight, his stubborn sense of duty, his ethics, his honor. And yet, she had been worn down by tragedy. If he could have prevented the buggy-whip lashing, why hadn't he? Was he trying to be a martyr to some cause? Did he care more for his pride than for his family?

She hated the termites of doubt and anger crawling through her, but she had had her fill of ethics and honor and duty and now wanted only for things to be as they were. He had become a stranger, almost frightening in his stiff ways. Couldn't he just think of her, or of the desperate children?

By the time she reached the warm kitchen, heady with aromas of the dearly bought ham, yeasty rolls in the oven, cloves and cinnamon, she could not conceal the tears.

"What's wrong, Mommy?" Rosalie asked.

"Everything," she replied and wished she hadn't said it.

"This is a bad Christmas."

"We will make it a good one. We are going to count our blessings and be glad about the Christ child coming to us."

"Birthdays should be happy," she said. "Can I go see Daddy?"

"He has a headache."

"How did he get hurt?"

"Oh, it was just an accident—" She stopped dead. She hated lies, even tiny ones. "Rosy, a man struck him with a whip."

"Was it Mr. Burch?"

"Yes, it was."

Rosalie turned away troubled, with pain in her small face. "I hope Mr. Burch won't whip me," she said.

"He would never whip a girl," she said.

Hannah turned to the oven to check on the small ham, and heard caroling outside, light, feminine voices tolling the old and joyous melodies. She hastened to the parlor window and saw a dozen adolescent girls bundled in scarves and wraps, many of them carrying candle lanterns, herded together by several adults. The girls turned toward the Knott porch, but the muffled adults—Hannah had no idea who—swiftly turned the girls away. There would be no joyous Christmas carols, no sharing of a neighborly moment, with the embezzler Knott and his family.

"Why didn't they sing for us?" Rosalie asked.

"Because . . . Christmas is not in them," Hannah said darkly. "If Christmas were in them, they'd sing extra carols for us and lift our hearts."

"It's because of the trouble. No one talks to us anymore."

It was true. Hannah's neighbors hurried by with averted eyes whenever she encountered them. No one paused for coffee or kitchen-table gossip. No one came to borrow an egg or return a cup. The Knotts still lived in Paradise, but it might as well have been the middle of the Sahara Desert.

Rosalie was crying. Hannah gathered the girl into her skirts, wondering how long she and the children could endure. And this was only the beginning.

A while later, she lit the candles against the terrible darkness outside and clambered wearily up the narrow stairwell to the half-story above, where she and Daniel occupied the front room and the children occupied the small slant-ceilinged rooms to the rear.

She opened the door onto darkness.

"Daniel?"

He sighed. She fumbled around, found a lucifer and lit the coal-oil lamp. He was staring at her, one eye almost swollen shut. He looked feverish.

"We're ready. I have our Christmas dinner."

He groaned.

"How are you, Dan?"

"Fever. Head driving me mad."

"We'll wait for you."

Seconds ticked by before he responded. "I can't."

"You have to. The children—"

"It's time they got used to Christmas without me," he said. "Unless things go better, there'll be a lot of holidays like that."

"But what shall I tell them?"

He didn't respond. She turned down the wick until the flame blued out and smoke caught in her nostrils.

"Tell them I've failed them."

"No, Dan. Do you really believe that?"

"I don't know what I believe anymore."

She reached across the darkness and pressed a hand to his forehead. It was burning. Then she walked out and closed the door behind her, sickened by what had come over her husband. She rousted the boys from their room and gathered her diminished and battered family around the Christmas table.

The world had shut them out. But she would tell her children that God never would.

Chapter 27

At first Eloise Joiner couldn't fathom what was happening to her that Christmas Eve, in her isolated ranch house up the valley from Paradise. Neither did she understand how she could feel two opposing emotions at the same time. For on the one hand she felt elation, as if she were a soaring eagle riding the updrafts. Yet on the other she felt anger and disgust. How could that make sense?

Her sole guest, the foremost luminary of southern Colorado, was being his smoothest and most charming self, exuding bland smiles and hearty cheer, very like a traveling lightning rod salesman. But she knew he was irritated and cranky and that he blamed her for the unpleasantness on the lonely road to town.

She had received so many compliments that evening from Amos his words seemed suspect, as if there was base metal under the silver-plating of his tongue.

"Ah, my dear Eloise, you've outdone yourself with this noble repast," he said. "A true Smithfield ham, succulent and tender, falling apart under tooth, two thousand miles from the smokehouse."

She just smiled and cleared the table. Compliments didn't transport dirty plates and cups to the dishpan or pop leftovers into the cold cellar or launder the linen napkins and tablecloth inherited from Rolf's mother, or scour the skillets and pots.

"Ah, beautiful Eloise, goddess of joy, Venus and Aphrodite and Diana and Helen, you are the embodiment of my fondest dreams, my heart's desire," he said, his voice amorous and husky, after she had piled the dishes into the pan to soak in hot water and yellow Fels Naptha flakes. She would scrub them later.

"Is that a proposal?" she asked, knowing exactly what he would say.

He turned solemn. "My dear, how I wish I could. Truly, you are my heart's desire. But of course that is impossible, and we must snatch happiness wherever we may."

"Why is it impossible?"

"Because of my position."

"Well, don't contest the divorce. Just let it go through, give Myrtle a settlement, and we'll be free to begin a life together."

"No, that must never happen. The ground she

chose is most unfortunate, and it behooves me to protect your honor and reputation."

"You mean *your* reputation."

"Well, that too, but I really am thinking of you."

"All right. If that's the problem, I'll solve it for you. I don't really care about my reputation. Let the world know I'm a fallen woman. I'm releasing you from your gallantry. I'm willing to brave the storms from all the pulpits in Paradise. I don't see the need for all this secrecy, these sealed court proceedings, and all. Once I would have cared, but no longer. So nothing's preventing you now. You're free to be candid to anyone who inquires."

Great furrows plowed his brow. "You mustn't take your reputation so lightly, Eloise. It's a cruel world, and gossiping tongues are hurtful tongues."

"It's all over town anyway, Amos. Courthouse people whisper, you know."

"No, it's not all over town. It won't ever be. I've seen to it. Myrtle's suit will be proven false and malicious and slanderous. It reflects upon me and my stewardship of Paradise. If anyone wishes to make an issue of it, I'll see him in court. I'll permit not one word of slander."

"And so you want me to live out here, alone, kept from society?"

"Ah, Eloise, my heart's desire is to free you from this rural prison altogether. But I lack the means."

"I don't like this scurrying around, these secret meetings. Maybe I'll reveal it myself."

"Eloise!"

"I might," she said, enjoying the fury and fear crawling across his face.

She settled back on the settee, listening to the crackle of wood in the stove.

"You have the means to marry me but not the will," she said. "It's really a simple matter. A divorce, a ceremony. Here I am, Amos. Take me!"

That irritated him, and she enjoyed it. Some odd, devilish instinct was driving her to turn the night that celebrated peace on earth into something contentious.

He seemed ill at ease. "You know, Eloise, I was here at the beginning. This town was even called Burchville for a few years, before I grew embarrassed. It was I who proposed to change it to Paradise, which perfectly expresses the aspirations of all our good citizens and solid families, and men of vision and skill. But as much as I yearned to place the burdens of leadership on others, they kept returning to my shoulders, perhaps because I own so much of the county. But also because, from the beginning, I lived as upright and honorable a life as I could."

"I guess maybe I should move, then," she said.

"What are you talking about?"

"I'm talking about leaving. Going away. Selling the ranch."

He looked shocked. "But why?"

"Because we are sneaking about. Because you're no longer living your ideals. Because I'm lonely out here. Because I'm hidden behind all your veils. Because, let's face it, Myrtle deserves her freedom. Because—"

"Enough! Let us not sully this sacred and holy evening."

But something heady was swirling about in her, some sense of pulling loose from a life she had come to hate.

"Yes," she said. "This is an evening to remember the good Lord. I was sorry I sent Daniel Knott packing this afternoon. He wants to clear his name."

"He shouldn't have come here. I told him if he did it again I'd put the sheriff on him."

"I might invite him. I found myself liking him."

"No, Eloise, you will *not* invite him."

"Amos, whose home is this?"

"The bank's."

"I will invite whomever I want to my hearth."

"Please, Eloise, I don't know what's come over you, but surely it's time to set it aside. This is going to be the sweetest and most beautiful night of my life, because I have you with me."

"Not mine," she said. Some wild mischief was blossoming in her, and she could no longer throttle it.

"It's time for you to try on another little gift I brought," he said, burrowing into his pocket.

"The night is young, Amos."

"Here," he said. He had a small jeweler's box in hand.

"An engagement ring?"

"Ah, no. Open it and see."

"Amos—the only thing I want is to come out of the shadows. I'm very lonely here. I'm pleased and flattered that you'd buy gifts so fine for me. I've never owned anything like that. My mother died when I was very small, and my father was a . . . wretch. My mother supported us, not him.

"But I remember her a little. She was much esteemed in our town, and I've been thinking of her tonight. I want what she had, the acceptance of people. Amos—I can't bear this sneaking around. Please understand. There is just one gift I want, and you can easily grant it just by owning up to what Myrtle is saying in court about us."

He shook his head.

"Yes, Amos! It would be a bad moment, but it would pass. People understand and forgive. You would never again have to pose as some sort of flawless mortal. And then the little box in your hand could contain the symbol of our betrothal and love, openly given and openly received."

She wondered where all that came from. Her mind had been dancing out of her control all afternoon. In fact, ever since Daniel Knott had come. It had taken only moments to realize that he hadn't wished to expose or hurt her or ruin her reputation; he only wanted to do what his soul required of him: to tell the exact truth under oath in Judge Boardman's court. And he believed so deeply in that that he was pitting his honor against everything that had fallen upon him.

Amos stared at her from eyes so dark they frightened her. It was as if he were raking her through his mind, looking for her weakness, rooting out her vulnerability.

But she would not retreat.

"I've gone to enormous lengths to protect you," he said in a grave manner that summoned sheer authority from within. "You have no idea what I've done to guard your honor. I've done something I'd never think of doing, just for you. I even arranged matters so that you didn't have to appear in court. I couldn't stop the deposition, but I was able to spare you an embarrassing ordeal on the stand. I put Alden on it, and he did what he could. Now you want to undo everything I did."

"And what exactly did you do?" The question lay grave and dark in the parlor.

"I cannot tell you. But that young man's testimony won't stand up. The word of a felon is not weighed heavily in any court."

Her pulse lifted wildly. What was he hinting at? Was everything that Daniel Knott had told her true? She had thought he was just inventing excuses to cover his criminal conduct. But now, suddenly, in the buttery light of the lamp, she knew that Daniel Knott was true and clean and fine as pure gold, had a soul as honest as sunlight, and that this man, this benefactor beside her on the settee, had plunged into an abyss.

"I found him to be just as plainspoken and honest as a man can be," she said tentatively, testing him.

"Nonsense! Eloise, what's come over you?"

"I believe him," she said tartly.

Burch stared. "What exactly do you believe?"

"That what's happened to him—the embezzlement charge . . ." Suddenly she was afraid and couldn't continue.

"You are so gullible."

She could not bring herself to talk for a moment, but suddenly words flowed out of her like spring water.

"You see, Amos, our honor is all we have," she said. "We have to like ourselves, but so many of us end up hating ourselves. I want you always to esteem yourself and to live in a way that you are esteemed by God, by friends and the community. But your friends are less important than your friendship with yourself."

He stared silently at her, and she knew her ideas were vanishing into a sea of ire.

Eloise stood. "Amos, I'm sorry this evening turned out badly for us. It was a mistake. I'll get your coat."

Her guest looked startled. She knew that absolutely no one in Archuleta County ever invited Amos Burch to leave.

He stood heavily. "It'll be a long, cold ride," he said. "I have made a mistake about you."

"Yes," she replied. "I am not what you want me to be. Ever since I gave that deposition, I haven't been able to live with myself."

"You'll live with it," he said. Was there a velvety threat in that?

She bundled the elegant coat back in its pasteboard carton and handed it to him, along with his gloves.

"Why?" he asked. "Why!"

She didn't reply. She couldn't bring herself to tell him that Daniel Knott had lit Advent candles in her soul. She had received a most beautiful and sacred Christmas gift from him.

Chapter 28

The squinty-eyed boy on the porch was unfamiliar to Daniel.

"You the bank robber?" he asked.

"No, I am not." Daniel started to shut the door.

"Hey, wait! You Dan Knott?"

Knott paused.

"Mrs. Burch sent me. She says you should come for a Christmas scone and tea."

"With Mrs. Knott?"

"Naw, she just said you."

"Right now?"

"I guess."

"Well, thank you."

"I wish I could rob a bank. I gotta wait until I'm grown."

Daniel shut the door hard.

He did not know whether he wanted to talk to Mrs. Burch. She and her attorney were at the heart of all his trouble. But he knew he had better heed the imperial request.

"Myrtle Burch wants to see me," he told Hannah. "But it's Christmas."

"The rich have their own calendars, I guess. I think I'd better go and find out what else is going to ruin me."

He approached the great white house warily, hoping he would not discover buggies and carriages in the oval drive. But as far as he could tell, she had no guests. He rapped on the gold-plated knocker sharply, and the servant, Mrs. Cutler, admitted him, pretending not to notice the angry welt across his cheek. She took his coat and scarf and hat and gloves and delivered him to a glowing yellow sunroom at the extreme southern end of the house. He marveled at the furniture, all of which had been brought by wagon from the two coasts. Nothing like this home existed elsewhere in the county.

He discovered Myrtle Burch before a fieldstone fireplace flanked by rising columns of glass that admitted the sulking winter sun.

She rose slowly, leaning on a silver-knobbed malacca cane. "Please come in, Mr. Knott. I'm so glad you could come. We shall have a Christmas visit—why, forgive my asking, but whatever happened to your cheek?"

"It was struck with a buggy whip."

She seemed to grasp more than had been said. "That's an evil wound. I hope you've seen a doctor."

"I don't have money for a doctor."

She paused, then plunged in again. "Mrs. Cutler will serve us tea and scones in just a moment."

He settled uncomfortably in a yellow silk wing chair and waited. This was obviously not a social visit.

"Yes, you're quite right," she said, reading his thoughts. "This is scarcely a social visit, is it? Now, we're quite alone. One of my sons, Dilworth, did make it here for Christmas, but he's now with his father at the bank. They plan to go duck hunting in the morning."

Knott nodded. "I'm glad you invited me. Is there something you wish to say to me?"

"There are things I wish to know. Eben Lytell says he can't tell me about you. Client confidentiality and all that. He's a very proper man, and I couldn't worm a thing out of him, so I decided to go straight to you."

He tried to grin, but the swollen cheek twisted it into pure pain. Mrs. Cutler returned with a sterling tea service on a bamboo cart, and retreated. Mrs. Burch did the honors, managing to pour the tea and flavor it, even with her gnarled hands, the joints of her fingers swollen to twice their normal size. Knott found himself with a teacup of Earl Grey, and some scones loaded with preserves. The ritual fascinated him.

"Now, then, Mr. Knott, I will tell you about my hopes and dreams. You might be surprised by them."

He sipped and waited, glad he did not have to talk.

"I want to return to my home and family in Hartford. I wish to do so unencumbered by any legal ties, such as separation, and with some security. Here I am, surrounded by all the comforts a woman could want—and yet the thing most precious to me is lacking. I'm married to a stranger, you see. He's been here all the while, physically present, at least until he moved to his suite at the bank a few months ago. But with my children grown, and no substance to my marriage, I began to yearn for my sisters and brothers, nieces and nephews, and the amenities of an old, gracious city where I grew up.

"But how? I proposed an uncontested divorce, but Amos would have no part of it. Mr. Lytell thinks that we may have new grounds, desertion, now that Amos is living at the bank. But up to now, the only possible ground has been his . . . wandering. So we proceeded, and I never dreamed my action would affect others."

"It's certainly affected me, ma'am."

She sighed and sipped her tea. "If you wish to do so, I would like to hear the entire story. I have a reason. And what you say I will hold in confidence."

"I'm not sure it's a good idea—"

"Well, I want you to tell me. The divorce action resumes in January, you know. Alden Streeter got a delay because of new evidence. That was your indictment, of course. Mr. Lytell is quite put out about it because it could mean your testimony will be thrown out and we'll lose. He hasn't quite said so, but I sense he doesn't believe a word of your story, and of course would rather that you weren't his client. But Prescott Boardman rules the roost." She smiled suddenly. "Mr. Knott, defend yourself to me. If you aren't an embezzler, tell me why. I do have a reason."

Knott wondered what additional trouble he was walking into. But he decided to go ahead. He was alone, represented by a lawyer who thought there was utterly no connection between the divorce testimony and what had happened at the bank, and he had nothing to lose.

So he began at the beginning and didn't stop until he had described his recent encounter with Burch on the lonely road and everything that Amos Burch had said.

"Well, do you believe it?"

She mulled over her words before answering. "It's hard to believe Amos would go to such lengths. I know him well. He's a good man at heart. No, it's just not like him. An elaborate and vicious forgery and fraud, putting a man in prison just to avoid gossip? No wonder you provoked him to anger. No, Mr. Knott. I know my husband and I know what lines he would never, ever cross. I wish I could believe your story . . ."

"I guess I'd better go."

"No, stay."

He stood. He would not let imperious ladies tell him when to sit or stand.

"Please let me pour you some tea. It's a luxury, you know. I get my Earl Grey shipped to me from Boston."

He sat down again. He had never felt so alone, so small against the giant forces operating against him.

"I don't know whether you're innocent or not, but I know Amos is being just as hard on you as he can be. It gnaws at me, you know. Even if I should win my freedom and go to Hartford, it would trouble me.

"Now, mind you, I'm not saying I believe you, or that the man I know so well would ever stoop to such desperate and cruel conduct. He's basically a good man with a keen conscience. I suspect you are, too, and all this bank business is simply a mistake, an error."

Knott sat quietly, not knowing what to say.

"Mr. Lytell says we'll probably lose the divorce suit because your testimony will be tainted by your conviction. Amos is in the driver's seat, you know. But tomorrow, Mr. Lytell is going to offer to settle. We'll agree to drop the divorce, with its adultery ground, if Amos agrees to a legal separation based on desertion. I just want you to know that."

He nodded, wondering what effect it would have. There was none that he could think of.

"I hope that'll help you," she went on. "Your testimony won't mean anything if we settle."

"Thank you, but it's too late."

"Maybe not," she said. "Let me think."

She rose, leaning on her malacca cane, which signaled the end of the interview, and he worked his way through the great house to its foyer. Much to his surprise, Mrs. Cutler handed him a pasteboard box of Christmas cookies at the door.

So that's what it came down to: he had satisfied a rich woman's curiosity.

Chapter 29

Daniel Knott waited for Horatio Bates to show up at the window. The postmaster seemed distracted, as if his mind was on other things and putting up the mail was the least of his interests.

But eventually Bates did shuffle out of his rear cubicle, surveying Knott at the window and shaking his head.

"Mail's delayed. There's snowslides between here and Ouray, and the coaches can't get through. Try later, eh?"

"I wasn't expecting anything."

"Time on your hands, eh?"

Bates was at it again. He was the nosiest man in Paradise, and Knott had a theory that he simply used his office as postmaster to fuel his curiosity and satisfy his penchant for gossip.

"Yes," Knott said and pulled his gloves on.

"You pine for a cup of week-old java?"

"I don't think so, Mr. Bates."

"I've been wanting to talk to you."

"About my difficulties, I suppose. I think not."

"I hear things. People talk in post offices, did you know that? They think I'm deaf. Actually, they forget I'm right here, sort of invisible to them, like a piece of furniture. That's what I suppose I am: furniture."

"What sort of furniture, Mr. Bates?"

"You got me there, Knott. I will scrub the pot and put it on the stove, and before you can tell me half your woes, I'll be pouring some fresh elixir of java bean down your gullet."

Knott had nothing to do. This day after Christmas, he had run out of ideas. He could no more defend himself in court than he could stop an avalanche by yelling at it. So he stepped around the small oaken gate that barred ordinary mortals from the holy precincts of the Unites States mail and found himself in Bates's lair, where he discovered more dark-stained cubbyholes than he had ever seen in his life.

Strewn on the postmaster's desk were items that reflected Horatio Bates's pursuit of a dozen lines of knowledge, ranging from a connoisseur's collection of perpetual-motion machines that didn't perpetuate, to an illustrated collection of wacky United States patents, including one that was intended to give the master of a house the means of ejecting a lazy wife from her bed by merely pulling a lever, to sets of English and American histories.

"Sit," he invited, while puttering with his coffee ritual. "Tell me what happened if you wish. If not, I'll talk."

"You talk," Knott said.

"All right. As I told Hannah, a postmaster hears things. I know all about the Burch divorce and your testimony, and how you stuck to your guns and Streeter couldn't shake you loose, not even a hair."

He chucked some piñon pine into the maw of the cast-iron potbellied heater and settled gingerly into his chair. "Hemorrhoids," he said. "It's the disease of the learned and the sedentary. The more you know, the worse your tail hurts."

"Which are you, learned or sedentary?"

"I think I'm the village idiot. So—did you do it?"

The question, fired so artfully and casually, caught Knott amidships.

"No. Nothing's missing from the bank."

"I thought so. I'm an amateur detective. I have some good information about John Wilkes Booth and Jack the Ripper."

Knott wondered whether he ought to escape this increasingly eccentric old bachelor.

"Let me make a theoretical case. Pure hypothesis, of course. Now, suppose that our leading light, the honorable Burch, didn't much like the idea of being caught with his britches around his ankles and using a lady for a cushion. Now suppose that he, being next to God in the general direction of omnipotence, decided to do something about it."

Much to Knott's astonishment, Bates had figured

out the underlying truth, getting the essentials right.

"Of course you didn't do it, Knott. He meant for the embezzlement stuff to be a lever, a crowbar. Only problem is, our local Archimedes discovered that you don't move, you don't lie, and you're more honorable than he ever dreamed of being. Have I got it right?"

"Yes."

"How'd he do it?"

"I don't know all of it. His hand is similar to mine. All he had to do was learn my capital letters, which are rounder than his. He did it so well that when I was shown the ledgers I thought it was my own hand. But they're frauds, intended to pressure me into altering my testimony. He never dreamed it would go this far. I was supposed to cave in. He's got my own ledgers hidden somewhere. I need both sets to prove my case. I don't know where my ledgers are or how to get them. But the last place they'd be is in his suite above the bank. Eben Lytell thinks I'm crazy even to suspect Amos C. Burch of such a thing."

"Do you expect anyone to believe you?"

"No. Unless I can show the court both sets, I'm sunk."

"Well, you'll have to get those records. Have Lytell subpoena them."

"We've already looked at the ledgers, under the bank's supervision."

"Have Lytell put Burch on the stand and start

asking about those records. It was Burch who discovered the fraud, wasn't it?"

"No, he had two Denver accountants auditing the books."

"Ah, he's a clever one. You could put the accountants on the stand, and what would they know but what they examined? Put Burch on anyway, eh?"

"Eben Lytell just won't do that. Not Burch. Remember, Lytell doesn't believe me. He thinks my whole story is a wild, half-baked cover-up of a crime. Mrs. Burch doesn't believe me either, and she knows her husband as well as anyone alive. It would violate his sense of honor and integrity, she said. Horatio, the stark truth is that no one believes me, except maybe Hannah, and I sense that even she's uncertain. About the time I'm sentenced and sent away, her faith in me just might crack, too."

"I believe you."

"What possible reason?"

"Oh, I've been around the town and over the hill, and I take to the study of character."

"You might as well believe in astrology."

"In fact, I don't. But I believe you."

Something tender bloomed in Daniel. At least someone believed him.

Bates picked up a hot pad, lifted the coffeepot from the stove, and poured Knott a blue-and-white-speckled tin cup of coffee.

"Now what are you going to do?" he asked.

Knott shrugged. He figured the less he said, the less would drift back to the ears of Amos C. Burch.

"You don't want to talk, but that's all right. In truth, I admire you. A man who can't be bent, and won't violate his conscience, is a man to toast with some good Dom Perignon. Why won't you end your ordeal?"

"I just won't."

"That's a good answer. No elaborate rationalizations. Just a gut-level instinct to do what's right. Well, you'll pay the price, I'll wager. And I'll tell you the price you're paying. You're the hottest topic out there in the lobby, so I know things that not even you know."

"Like what?"

"You're more isolated than you know. I don't think there's a soul, myself excepted, who supposes you're innocent. They want you up for as many years as the law allows, if they don't lynch you first."

"Lynch?"

"I've heard talk, but no one's actually going to do it. That's just people getting mean. Most people don't even know about the divorce and the adultery and your testimony. The paper's never tattled on its owner, and the few who do know keep it quiet because the town's leading light has a dozen ways to hurt them if they don't. But everyone else, right down to four-year-olds and immigrants who don't speak six words of English, they know about you and the bank.

"By the time this is over, and Judge Boardman sends you away, you'll be entirely alone, save for me. Burch is in too deep to stop this. He didn't mean for this to happen. He never imagined he'd run into a stubborn cuss like you, who wouldn't bend an inch, and now he's trapped by his own lies. He's going to feel bad about it; he's chock-full of virtue, except when it's inconvenient to be virtuous, and it's going to haunt him. But that's no consolation for you.

"But if you stand it, and don't budge, maybe some good things will result. I like to think there's justice in the world, but sometimes it's delayed a piece. If you stand up and stay true to yourself and your honor, only good'll come of it.

"Good men are sacrificed all the time by people who prefer expediency. When you get right down to extremes, it's between you and God. If you and God know you're innocent, that's worth a life. The whole world can condemn you, but they don't have power over you.

"You're one of a kind, Daniel—at least if I read you right you are, and I think I do. You've got courage and strength, and no man can take those things away. They can take your freedom, and even your life, but they can't take away truth.

"So you just stand up and be proud, and keep on fighting, even if those closest to you—and I'm thinking of Eben Lytell—don't believe a word and want you to bargain for a reduced sentence or leniency, want you to be 'reasonable.' You have to say no and keep on trusting."

"I don't have that kind of strength, Horatio," Knott said. "I'm just an ordinary man who got trapped, and I'm at the end of my rope."

Chapter 30

December slid into January and the embezzlement trial loomed ever closer. Amos Burch's attorney received another postponement of the divorce proceedings, arguing that Knott's conviction for embezzlement would impeach his testimony in Myrtle Burch's divorce proceedings.

Daniel Knott lived in a nightmarish world in which he and his family were pariahs, isolated, unable to buy anything but food. The children's wounds only deepened as the result of the cruelties they experienced at school. Hannah had become frayed and short-tempered.

Daniel discovered that Eben Lytell was intent upon reducing the sentence rather than building a case.

"You don't believe my story, so why do you represent me?" Knott said one cold January morning.

"I'm doing the only thing possible for you. You

have no criminal record, and you have a family, and I'm going to try to get the minimum for you."

"But I didn't do it."

"They've shown us the books. In your hand."

"It wasn't my hand. It's Burch's forgery of my hand."

Lytell laughed. "Prove it," he said.

"At least let me tell my story in court," Knott replied.

"I don't want you on the stand telling that inane story. It'll make things worse for you, throwing mud on your employer. Are you really going to sit there and tell a jury that Amos Burch was so offended by your divorce testimony, and so intent on forcing you to change it, that he forged bank documents and threatened to destroy you if you didn't change it?"

"Yes."

"And do you know how the court'll respond?"

"I will trust my peers to hear me out."

"And you're aware of Amos Burch's reputation here?"

Knott nodded. "Just put me on and let me talk," he said.

Lytell shook his head. "I am doing my best to ease the sentencing. You're going to do your best to get the maximum. There's only one other possibility: an accounting error. Are you sure you didn't make mistakes?"

"There was no mistake."

"That's something the jury would buy. Mistakes are understandable."

"Every night I balanced and checked my books and examined my day's work. I rarely made miscalculations."

Lytell shook his head.

And that was how it went every time Knott and Lytell got together.

Things went bad at home, too. Hannah turned cold and silent. She no longer offered supportive words, and he knew she was close to despair.

The *Paradise Tattler* only made things worse, with a story in each of its biweekly editions.

TRIAL LOOMS

The trial of alleged embezzler Daniel Knott is slated to begin January 7, according to Henry Cobble, clerk of district court.

Knott has been indicted for peculations totaling over nine thousand dollars from the Merchant Bank. The bank's chief officer, Amos Burch, assures bank depositors that the losses will be fully covered and all deposits are safe.

"We have attached Knott's property, and expect to recover most of the money as soon as the criminal proceedings are over."

Burch said he believes the evidence is substantial and will persuade the jury to render a guilty verdict. The crime carries a prison sentence ranging up to fifteen years . . .

The paper never approached Knott and never asked for his side of the story. Knott figured that a paper owned by Amos Burch never would. So as the clock ticked, the town's citizens were given only just one side of the story, and Knott knew the jail doors would soon close upon him, and upon his freedom.

Hannah braced him early in the new year. "I'm going to Denver. I'm taking the children. They can't bear this. Day after day in school . . ."

"How will you pay to get there?"

"With my ring."

Daniel sensed that once the ring was off Hannah's finger, he would never be able to put his marriage back together.

"Would you wait until the trial is over? I'd want the children to leave if I lose. But I'd like to think people of this town won't judge me before the trial's over."

"But they already have."

Her tone was so bitter that he stared at her. "Do you believe I'm innocent?"

She averted her eyes. "Yes," she said tonelessly.

And then he knew he had lost her, too.

She looked terrible. Great black bags puffed out under her eyes. She had lost weight. The brightness had vanished from her visage.

And he could still change all that with a few small lies under oath. The knowledge of it tore him to shreds.

One day a gang of boys caught Rosalie, escorted her to a "jail" they had constructed from old crates, and held her there in the dark, cramped, cold, taunting her all the while. They threw whatever came to hand at their prisoner, splashing her with mud and bruising her with rocks, but it was the words they threw that pierced her heart.

They didn't let her go until dusk, when their mothers were putting dinner on the table. She walked home, mute, filthy, and frightened. It took Hannah all evening to worm the story out of her, and then she soothed her, held her, crooned lullabies, and lay beside her until she fell into a troubled sleep.

From that hour, Hannah turned stony eyes on Daniel.

He took to hiking, arguing with himself, finding reasons to surrender, alter the testimony and be done with it. It would be the loving thing to do. It would stop this torment. Burch would no doubt discover the "mistake" in the bank records and that would be over. All Knott had to do was cooperate. But he couldn't. He just couldn't.

On one of those tormented perambulations, well outside of town, Burch's black buggy slowed and stopped beside him. The hood was up, protecting Burch from the cruel weather.

"Get in," Burch said.

Wearily, Knott settled beside the man who was tormenting him.

"Fine horse, El Morocco. He loves a raw day like this. I can hardly hold him back," Burch said. "You healed up yet?"

"No."

"Too bad. You drove me beyond my habit of temperance. You ready for fifteen years?"

"No."

"I didn't think so. It's not too late, you know. Spare your people."

"It was too late the day after I testified at your divorce action."

"Myrtle's lawyer came to us: she'll drop the adultery ground if I accept separation with desertion as a ground. Streeter laughed in their face, you know. The adultery ground won't ever be proven. Your testimony won't be worth a thing. They're desperate. Myrtle wants to get out, but she's going to stay married.

"I won't let her go. We're the first couple of Paradise, and we'll smooth things over, and we'll keep up standards for the sake of the whole town. She can't make a desertion case. I pay all the bills and visit her once a week. And that's why her divorce petition won't be granted."

"Then why do you pressure me?"

"I don't want your testimony on the record."

"But if it's the testimony of an embezzler, what difference will it make?"

"I won't stand for a whisper against my character."

"You asked me to sit here. What do you want?"

"Time's running out, Knott. You just volunteer to amend and amplify your testimony—that's what the lawyers call it. It's not even a retraction. It's done all the time. On reflection, you weren't sure who you saw, maybe it was the cordwood man, anything like that. And maybe things'll go better for you."

"Maybe?"

"It's not too late for me to discover that the bank's books are sound. Of course, we'd still have to let you go. I won't have you there. But you'd be out of court. And you could leave Paradise."

"I'm ruined regardless."

"Yes. And you brought it on yourself, you stubborn cuss. I've never met such a fool."

Knott stared into the low winter light. "No, Mr. Burch, I won't lie, not even to save myself fifteen years. My entire conduct has been honorable and truthful. I'm made of better stuff than you. When the test came, I stood like a man, but you . . . you're a fraud and a forger. The sad thing is, you're a good man, an honorable man in all save this."

"Get out."

He tugged the lines, and El Morocco slowed and stopped.

"No, not until I've said my say. You weren't expecting this, were you? You were going to talk to me, but you didn't expect me to talk back. Well, I haven't quit and I never will.

"The trouble is, in all other things you're a benefactor and a model for this town. People love that Burch. They would quickly forgive the Burch I know. But now you've smeared yourself. You'll be here in Paradise, loathing yourself, hating what you did to me, hating what you've done to your marriage, ashamed of this betrayal of everything you've ever stood for.

"And for what? Because you violated your marriage vows? That's bad, but it doesn't bring other men's worlds down on their heads. Think of it. I'll be imprisoned for a long time, knowing I'm innocent. Every day I'm in there, I'll be able to hold my head high. As much as I'll hurt, I won't have chains on my soul.

"And you? You'll be imprisoned for the rest of your life by your conscience, your violated sense of honor, your own sense of decency. By the time you're an old man, you'll be the most miserable creature alive, awaiting the judgment of God, eaten alive with remorse. Your life's going to turn to ashes."

Amos Burch sat silently, slumped in the buggy seat.

"It's your choice, not mine," Knott said.

Burch tried to regain whatever had fled from him, sitting upright, controlling the trembling of his hands, but he said nothing. He just stared at Knott with eyes that radiated pain and defeat.

"I'll walk home," Knott said gently. He stepped out of the buggy and left Amos C. Burch sitting on the country road, going nowhere.

Chapter 31

Eloise Joiner parked her spring wagon right in front of the Merchant Bank. It was a novelty that she enjoyed after months of hiding her presence in town. She wrapped the lines around the hitching post, knowing Old Blue wouldn't go anywhere anyway, and walked into the sunny building.

She approached Jasper Pickering and asked him to withdraw her balance.

"You going somewhere, Mrs. Joiner?"

"Yes," she said, leaving his curiosity unsatisfied.

It didn't come to much. He showed her the ledger balance—$33.08—and paid it out in greenbacks and coin, entering zeros as the remaining balance.

"If you want to reopen it, just let me know," he said.

She tucked the bills and coins into her reticule. "Is Amos in his office?" she asked.

"Right back there."

She traced her way through the little gate and down the aisle to his open door.

He looked up, startled.

"Eloise! I thought you knew never—"

"Yes, never to come here. But this is bank business."

He swung around his waxed desk and closed the door, sealing them off from the world. Then he retreated to his swivel chair, obviously in a dour mood.

She settled in the chair opposite and let him stew for a moment. Things had come to a head, and she had made some large decisions.

"I'm going to sell the ranch and leave," she said.

"But, Eloise—"

"It's my decision, not yours."

"You can't do that! Your mortgage is higher than your ranch is worth. There's been a decline . . ."

"I can do it. I'm going to advertise, and if no one buys it I'll turn it over to the bank."

"I see," he said, frowning. "That is ill-advised."

"No, it's not. Staying there after I was widowed and alone was ill-advised. What I'm doing is the first sensible thing I've done in two years. If you want to buy it, you can bid on it."

"I have a cattle lease."

"I'm not aware that I've signed anything or that we've ever discussed it, other than saying that you'd put your herd on and pay me monthly."

He settled into his chair, his face a mask. "I suppose this somehow has to do with your present un-happiness."

"It has to do with you. I have no intention of living in isolation as your secret paramour out there, supported by your checks."

"You'll end up with nothing, Eloise. This is utter foolishness."

"No, I'll have one thing: my honor." She watched him absorb that. "I don't suppose that means anything to you anymore. Honor isn't money and has no cash value. You once treasured it, and your good name. And I value it more than I value wealth. And do you know who inspired me to cleanse my soul? Daniel Knott."

"What has he to do with it?"

"I believe he told the truth, no matter what you threw at him. You'll send him to prison now on trumped-up charges because he wouldn't bend or break."

"Where did you get that notion?"

"You as much as said so Christmas Eve. You said you'd pressure him until he amended his testimony. Didn't you?"

"I don't recollect it."

"It's quite plain to me what you're doing to an honorable man. That's why I'm leaving. That's why you'll never touch me again."

"Careful what you say, Eloise."

"Don't threaten me. What's become of you, Amos Burch? Why have you abandoned your own conscience?"

"I have a grazing lease, an oral one, to be sure, and I'm afraid I'll have to act to protect my interests if you leave me."

"If I walk away from here with nothing but the clothing I wear, I'll be better off than you. And if you wonder how I came to that, it was because I learned about honor from Daniel Knott."

"He's an embezzler."

She laughed derisively as she stood and turned to leave. "I'm going to advertise. If you want the ranch, bid on it."

She stepped out of the bank into juniper-scented air and felt suddenly, deliriously free. She wasn't even shaking. Honor had armored her against the dread she had expected. She felt so many emotions that she couldn't sort them out. Amos Burch was a tender, well-educated, generous man who had helped her. Or once was. They had shared blissful moments. She remembered their intimacies with delight. She didn't deny the regrets that now welled in her heart. If Amos hadn't taken his bad turn, she might still be enjoying him.

She stopped at the *Tattler* and arranged for a small notice putting her ranch up for sale for three thousand or best offer, paid eleven dollars to run it for a month, and then headed for the offices of Eben Lytell.

The next task was going to be the hardest part of all, one that could result in a fine and imprisonment for perjury. But the vision of Daniel Knott inspired her. If he could do it, whatever the cost, so could she.

She discovered that the young attorney was with a client, so she waited patiently in the foyer of his home. She could hear the rise and fall of muffled voices in the parlor, and after twenty minutes a limping ranch hand emerged and left.

Lytell was surprised at her presence. "You have some business with me, Mrs. Joiner?"

She nodded, entered the austere offices, and settled into a battered wooden chair.

He sat down, expectantly. "Well?" he asked.

She couldn't speak. The words rushed to her throat and halted there. She suddenly wanted to flee.

He eyed her and tapped his desk with a pencil. "Is it about the divorce, or have you other business?"

She knew she was reddening. "The divorce," she said brusquely.

Time ticked by. He looked restless.

"Perhaps you've reconsidered what you came to tell me. Would you like to come back some other time? I'm pretty busy."

"I'll talk. Please give me a moment to compose myself."

She felt her pulse lift. "I lied under oath."

It hung there. The pencil stopped tapping.

"I didn't want to in the first place. I was pressured—oh, God, every word was given to me as if I was in a Punch and Judy show."

She was grateful that he said nothing. But his gaze seemed to penetrate her innermost soul.

"Amos and I . . ." The tears rose unbidden. She dabbed at her wet cheeks. "I don't know how it started. He offered to help me when I, when the bank, the foreclosure, when I needed . . . the payment. He helped me, gave me six hundred dollars—six hundred! And he stayed one afternoon, and it . . . You don't know how hard this is. I am . . . I'd never ever dreamed of doing anything like that. I've always been faithful, and I never . . ."

She dabbed at her eyes.

"You and Amos were lovers?"

"Yes. And Mr. Knott found us. I never dreamed someone from the bank would walk into his office at night. And I lied because—because I was weak and I let Amos tell me what to say, and I didn't want to lose my reputation. Now I'll go to prison."

"Maybe not. The trial isn't over, and you can usually amend your testimony at this point and not be cited."

"But it's not just an amendment, it's a retraction."

"Was anyone else involved in falsifying the facts?"

"No. I mean, you asked the questions, but only Amos told me what to say."

"You weren't coached by Mr. Streeter?"

She shook her head. "I'm so sorry. I've tried to be a good person . . ."

"You are a good person. And you have tremendous courage."

"I didn't until I saw Daniel Knott suffering and not bending an inch. Then I knew what courage is."

"What did Amos Burch tell you to say?"

She told him about Amos's deceits, which formed a web of half-truths. Yes, she had come into town to shop. Yes, she had stayed overnight at the hotel.

"But it was all a deception, and I hated it then and hate it now, even worse than ruining my reputation."

He smiled suddenly. "Sometimes, Mrs. Joiner, these things make reputations rather than ruin them. Will you testify voluntarily to all this when the divorce case resumes? This would give Myrtle Burch what she wants, as well as great happiness."

"Yes," she whispered.

He questioned her further, taking notes this time, and then rose.

"But there's more," she said.

That puzzled him, but he shrugged and waited.

"On Christmas Eve I was visited first by Daniel Knott and then by Amos. Daniel asked me to corroborate his testimony. He told me a terrible story about Amos, and the trumped-up embezzlement."

"Yes, I've heard it. It's the ranting of a man who has no defense. I've heard dozens of criminals rave like that. Excuses, crazy stories."

"But it's true! They'd had an encounter on the road and when Amos arrived at my place, he was severely angry. He talked about it, too. He told me he was putting pressure on Knott, that he would break him and make him retract the divorce testimony. He said he was doing it for me, to save my reputation, and that he didn't want it on the record, and he'd do whatever it took. He didn't say how, but he said he would. He admitted it!

"That did it. That's when everything fell into place. I told him it wasn't for me but for himself that he was doing this. It wasn't my reputation he was trying to salvage. He said it was for the good of the town. That was when I knew I had to escape this place, escape him. I wanted to be as good and fine and true and courageous as Daniel Knott is. If I'm now a scarlet woman, I can't help that, but at least I'm telling the truth."

Eben Lytell stared at her. "Are you saying that Daniel Knott's wild tale is true? That Knott didn't rob the till? That Amos Burch would do all that to him? *Amos Burch?* Just to hide an adultery? Tell me the whole story again, slowly, leaving nothing out," he said.

She did, and the tears came, but so did release. A thousand pounds had floated off her shoulders.

Chapter 32

Daniel Knott found himself in unending midnight. Hannah was doubting him. One night she asked him to please, please, confess his crime; she had to know.

All he could do was tell her, quietly, that he had never taken a thing from the bank. She just turned away.

She tried escorting the children to school and home again, but that didn't stop the cruelties of others, who taunted them along the way. So she withdrew Rosalie altogether and tried to continue with a *McGuffey's Reader* at home. But the girl stared into space, unable to focus.

His whole family was suffering and he was helpless to stop it. He was no longer tempted to lie. Once he resolved to stick to the truth as he knew it, the pressure vanished. He was reconciled to his fate, and he understood that soon he would never see the sun except through cold iron bars.

The only comfort he received came from Horatio Bates, who often dragged him into his rear office and peppered him with anecdotes and illustrations.

"Daniel emerged from the lion's den," he said. "You'll emerge from this graced by the finger of God."

But Knott saw no finger of God stirring the world in Paradise, Colorado. His innate piety was so battered and drained that he found no comfort at all in the idea that at least God knew the truth, or that God even cared.

Then, shortly before the trial, Eben Lytell summoned him. Knott went reluctantly, knowing that the skeptical lawyer wanted only to mitigate the sentence. But this time things were different.

Lytell actually smiled and invited Knott to sit down.

"I believe you," he said.

That so astonished Knott that he could find no answer.

"It's a hard story to believe, isn't it? I'm going to tell your story to the court, exactly as you told it to me."

"Why?"

"Mrs. Joiner came in yesterday and confirmed everything you've said, not only in the divorce matter but about the pressures that Burch put on you. I could scarcely believe it.

"Amos Burch is such an innately good man I've

had trouble believing he possesses even the smallest
flaw. But that's absurd. Who of us is perfect? It's just
that, year after year, there he's been, talking to
schoolchildren about morality, reading the Scripture
lessons in church, setting the tone, making Paradise
a town that's reaching, stretching its arms toward
whatever virtue can be achieved short of heaven.
But I've been blind, Daniel."

Knott felt the stirrings of something, but it wasn't
hope. He had been beyond hope for so long now.

"Eloise Joiner said she lied in the deposition; that
you were right. You caught the two of them. She
said that after you visited her on Christmas Eve,
pleading for help, Burch showed up as angry as a
hailstorm and told her flatly that he was pressuring
you and would continue to do so until you snapped
or bent to his will. He didn't tell her what exactly he
was doing, but that was obvious to her. She'll testify
to these things, and I will call her."

"Does that make my case, Mr. Lytell?"

"Unfortunately, no. She's admitting that she lied
under oath, and Erich Braunfels—he'll be the one
prosecuting this case—is going to go after that and
destroy everything she says about you and Amos
Burch. The testimony of an admitted liar isn't going
to help much. I'll try to elicit from her the coaching
she got from Burch before she did the deposition,
but it probably won't do much good. Amos Burch is
simply untouchable in this town. And the jury is
probably going to believe Braunfels. He'll find mo-

tives, and try to prove that both of you had quarrels with Saint Amos."

Knott felt his spirits sag again.

"Let's go over this bank business again," Lytell said.

"I know that Burch forged some ledgers and showed the forgeries to the outside auditors."

"You can't prove it?"

"Burch must be hiding the real pages somewhere—if we could only find them."

"Are these mortgage ledgers in a bound volume? Did he have to forge an entire volume?"

"No, they were separate pages in files. When a mortgage is paid off, we put it into an expandable ledger book for the permanent record."

"So Burch had only to doctor a few pages to put you in trouble?"

"Yes. When I saw these, I thought they were in my own hand."

"We can go study them. Maybe there's something we can spot. Where would you think he'd hide the true ledger pages?"

"Nowhere that would connect him to the pages. Not in his upstairs suite, not in the bank safe or in his home. He's too smart."

"We need those pages. Think about it. You've worked with him for years. You must have some ideas."

"I don't."

"What about in his many businesses? The grain business? The mercantile, the ranches?"

"That's where I'd look. They're all under managers. But he's got what, twenty businesses and ranches?"

Lytell sighed. "There's one other possibility. The county attorney's going to put Burch on to describe how the embezzlement was discovered, step by step. The outside accountants, too. That's going to be my one chance, Daniel. And it's risky. If I go an inch too far, the jury's going to stuff its ears with cotton and quit listening to our side. But I'll risk it."

"It doesn't sound good."

"All right, let's walk over to the courthouse. They'll have to produce those records. Braunfels has them. We're going to take a closer look."

Knott managed a smile. "For the first time, I don't feel so alone," he said.

Lytell sighed. "I'm sorry I came to this view so late. I'm a fighter and I'll make something of this. Whether I can spring you, I don't know."

Lytell steered toward the Merchant Bank, much to Knott's consternation. "We're going to start right here, Daniel," he said. "Let me do the talking."

Knott entered the bank with dread. They were greeted with dead silence.

"You look ravishing, Miss Gustafson," Knott said. He smiled.

She stared. Then, slowly, she smiled back, like a rose blossom unfolding. Someday some man would discover that Miss Gustafson was an American Beauty.

Lytell headed for Burch's office, but the bank's

president wasn't in. "All right, who's in charge?" he asked Pickering.

"I am, sir."

"We're going to look at records."

"But you can't. It's not allowed."

"It'll spare you a subpoena. We're going to see those records anyway. I want to see your entire loan files."

Pickering, not known as a tower of determination, pursed his thin lips and crumbled. "We'll have to watch you," he said, irritably.

"Sure, stand over us. Prevent us from performing villainies, sleight of hand, or any prestidigitation, Mr. Pickering."

Pickering brought the mortgage files to the mahogany worktable and hovered about, looking squinty.

"All right, Daniel, show me what everything means," Lytell said.

Slowly Knott worked through the files, the applications, the mortgage contracts, the ledgers, and the correspondence. They were written in various hands, but all used the same black ink and were penned on standard bank ledger forms.

"Show me one of yours," he said.

Knott picked out several mortgages he had prepared.

"Now, are there any that Burch set up himself? I want to look at his hand."

Knott remembered some and showed them to Lytell.

"I don't see much resemblance," he said.

Knott dipped a nib into an inkpot and wrote out some capital letters. "This is how I write them. This is how Burch writes them. Now put your finger over a capital and see if the lowercase letters look alike. See? They do. His capital *M* and his *W* are sharp and pointed. Look at mine—rounder, without those little wings. But the lowercase words look very similar."

"I see," said Lytell after studying the texts. "We'll subpoena these. They'll help."

They examined loan documents for an hour, while Pickering droned over them like a housefly. Then Lytell insisted on examining every file in the bank. Pickering wrung his hands, but let him.

"The safest place to hide something is in plain sight," Lytell said. "So we're going to see what's in plain sight."

"What are you looking for?" Pickering asked.

"Evidence," Lytell said.

"Well, you can't just look at everything in a bank."

"I'm not. I'm looking for mortgage documents that may be misfiled. I won't peek at a single private account."

"Nothing in this bank is misfiled, Mr. Lytell."

Lytell ignored him. One by one he opened file drawers looking for a sheaf of mortgage ledgers, but finding nothing.

"Are there any other files?"

"In Mr. Burch's office. I can't—"

Lytell retreated. "Just show me which file cabinet. I'll need a subpoena to access the files anyway."

"In his desk, and that file," Pickering said.

"All right. Thank you."

They stepped out into a blustery snow squall. "Unless Burch is crazy, he isn't going to keep incriminating documents inside his desk," Lytell said. "But I'll have a look."

At the courthouse, Lytell argued his way into an examination of the evidence, which Braunfels permitted only in his eagle-eyed presence. There, spread out on a table, were the incriminating ledger pages.

This time Eben Lytell was strictly silent, and Knott stayed silent too. Lytell whipped through the ledgers, one by one, finally pausing. There, in a heading of one of them, was a tiny clue: an *M* with sharp points and little wings. Lytell pointed. Knott nodded. Lytell wrote down the bank number and description of the document. One tiny slip of the pen. That was all they found. But it was enough.

"Thanks, Erich," he said, wrestling himself into his greatcoat. "Very helpful."

Braunfels laughed softly. "Sure, Eben. If you rub the evidence together, a genie gives you three wishes."

Chapter 33

Hannah Knott sat disconsolately in the overheated courtroom, almost unable to bear the spectacle before her eyes. The place reeked of sweat and fear. The jury had been selected that morning, and she studied these chosen men. Most of them had accounts at the Merchant Bank. She knew few of them, but Daniel probably knew them all. She dreaded the presence of Victor Malcolm, the owner of the general store, in that panel.

There Dan was, in that small box, so terribly alone. She ached for him. He would either leave that box a free man or be taken away and out of her life. She hurt because she had doubted him. Hurt because in his moment of deepest need she had pulled away, uncertain, angry, resentful that he couldn't bend a little and stop this torture of his family. Now remorse flooded her and brought tears to her eyes. But it was too late. He had spent his last free days crouched in a corner like a wounded animal, but she had not bound his wounds or helped him in the least.

Myrtle Burch sat quietly, her face blank, stoic. As far away from her as possible, Amos Burch sat erect, his eyes like black shotgun bores pointing at the world, menacing everything in his line of sight.

The prosecutor, Braunfels, made the people's case smoothly. He put the Denver auditors on and during the direct examination elicited a detailed description of the audit, the discovery of irregularities, the additional search that revealed dummy accounts, all in Knott's hand, and the interest-rate manipulation. Braunfels carefully introduced the assorted bank ledgers as evidence. Brick by brick by brick, the people's case was built.

He called upon Burch, who testified that the manipulation apparently ceased when Knott got his raise and promotion, evidence of a motive. He testified that Knott had shown promise, and that was why Burch had taken the important step of elevating him to a top position in the bank.

"I trusted that fellow—trusted him with every last cent in the Merchant Bank," he said.

Hannah thought that Burch looked terrible. His expression was so bleak and dark, his testimony so gravelly and brusque—he seemed to be suffering in some sort of private hell. But he never wavered in his condemnation of Daniel.

Eben Lytell chose to cross-examine Burch, asking several questions that didn't seem important to

Hannah. Had Burch alerted the auditors to possible fraud? No. How was it known that the ledgers were in Knott's hand? Because he did the mortgage accounting as his regular duty. But didn't Burch himself ever do some of the accounting? Only rarely. Didn't Burch's own hand look much like Knott's? Burch glared, then denied it. Had he or the auditors looked at the handwriting of everyone else connected with the bank? No. Then why had everyone supposed the ledgers in evidence were in Knott's hand? Weren't Burch's lowercase letters much like Knott's?

"They don't look a bit alike," he said.

"What's different about them?"

"I haven't the faintest idea. I would have to have samples before me," he said.

"We will provide some later. Why did you use different auditors on this occasion?"

"To save some money," he said.

"How much?"

"I don't have the invoices before me, Mr. Lytell."

"Please estimate how much."

"Ten percent."

This went on endlessly. Daniel sat grimly, listening to Amos put forth these terrible lies.

Eventually, Lytell put Daniel on the stand. Daniel was sworn in and settled sternly in the witness chair. He still seemed so alone, but Hannah could see something strong and resolute in him. He would endure, like granite, against all of nature's ferocity.

"Mr. Knott, we're going to tell the jury your story.

It's a remarkable story, filled with courage and honor, devotion to duty and uncompromising rectitude," Lytell began.

During his direct examination, he led Daniel into the divorce testimony—and immediately ran into trouble.

"Immaterial and irrelevant," objected Braunfels. "The proceedings of any other case before this court have nothing to do with this criminal proceedings."

"But they do. Our entire defense depends on it."

"Counsel will approach the bench," Judge Boardman said, and Hannah could hear only a low drone. She could see Lytell looked upset and argued vociferously.

But Boardman sustained the objection. "The jury will disregard any reference to any other legal proceeding. It must not color your verdict. Counsel will limit direct examination to the charges brought in the indictment."

"Your Honor," said Daniel, "I need to tell my story to defend myself. Let me tell it all in my own words."

"You are out of order, Mr. Knott. No more outbursts."

Hannah sensed that something horrible for her husband's defense had transpired.

Eben Lytell was not a man to let the ruling pass, and he tested it at every opportunity. But Braunfels was vigilant and objected whenever Daniel tried to relate his tale. She watched the jury, which was plainly becoming bored and restless.

After that, everything seemed to disintegrate. She watched, heartsick, as Daniel struggled to tell his story without being able to explain Burch's motive. There he was, saying that the town's most beloved and generous and morally upright citizen had engaged in a despicable fraud to pressure him. "Objection, objection!" Braunfels shouted.

He tried to recount Burch's two contacts with him, once on the valley road and once in the closed buggy, but the moment he alluded to the divorce testimony, all Hannah heard was, "Objection, immaterial."

Erich Braunfels made quick work of him during the cross-examination, smiling, evoking laughs, stabbing deep and hard, making Daniel's testimony look ludicrous. Daniel suffered all that resolutely, with an odd dignity, as if shielded by his private thoughts. Her heart rushed out to him. He seemed somehow larger and more formidable than anyone else in the courtroom.

Lytell did no better with Eloise Joiner on the stand. He asked her what her relationship was to Burch.

She took a deep breach. "Lover," she whispered.

Prescott Boardman looked startled.

Braunfels objected. "I fail to see how that is germane," he said.

But this time, Boardman overruled the prosecutor.

"Did Amos Burch spend Christmas Eve with you at your ranch house?" Lytell continued.

"Yes."

"Did you talk about Daniel Knott?"

"Yes."

"What did he say?"

"He told me he was trying to protect us both, save me from embarrassment. That he was putting all the pressure he could on Knott to retract his testimony in the divorce—"

"Objection. Immaterial."

That resulted in another hushed conference with the judge. When it broke up, Lytell was visibly upset.

"The jury will disregard the testimony, or any testimony pertaining to any other proceedings," Boardman said. "The jury is instructed to weigh only such evidence as pertains to the alleged embezzlement."

So it had come to that. Not even Eloise Joiner's brave corroboration of Daniel, done at terrible cost to her own future, would be on the record.

That left the case of the capital *M*. Lytell successfully introduced documents written by Amos Burch and Daniel Knott, showing the distinctions in their treatment of capital letters, and then he put Burch on the stand once again.

He plucked up the ledger alleged to have been written by Knott. "Mr. Burch, this is one of the ledgers your auditors have said pointed the finger of guilt at Daniel Knott. But you will note that the capital *M* here is written in the way you write it, not in the way that Knott writes it. Did you write this ledger?"

Burch glared. "What nonsense!"

"Please answer the question."

"I won't stoop to that."

"Amos," said Judge Boardman, "yes or no."

"No."

"Who else in the bank might have written it?"

"Knott was in charge of mortgage accounting. So it must be his work."

"Are you very sure?"

"Yes."

"Does this replace any other ledgers not presented to this court?"

"Of course not."

"Then how do you account for this capital *M*?"

"I don't know. You're making much about nothing."

The jury wasn't very interested. Hannah could see that. A capital *M* wasn't going to change their minds.

She listened desolately to Erich Braunfels' cheerful closing argument, reminding the jury that Daniel Knott was accusing the town's benefactor and moral arbiter of fraud, forgery, and other heinous conduct, all as part of an obvious and desperate cover-up of his own stealthy peculations.

"This guttersnipe is accusing Amos Burch of a dozen crimes! I rather enjoy it, myself. Knott himself makes the people's case!"

He laughed at the whole defense, ridiculed the detail of the capital letter *M*, asked what possible motivation Burch could have to pressure an em-

ployee, and assured the veniremen that not only
should they convict, but they also should cleanse
away the mud that had splattered Amos C. Burch.

"Drive this serpent out of Paradise!" he concluded loftily.

Lytell faced a daunting task. Hannah watched
him study the jury, looking for ways to raise doubts
about Burch's conduct, reminding the jurors that if
they had any reasonable doubt they could not convict. He managed to feed more about Daniel's divorce testimony into the summation, while Prescott
Boardman scowled. But it went badly, and the jurors squirmed.

Amos Burch stared blackly, his face hardened into
stone, through it all. Myrtle looked pale and disturbed. Boardman listened patiently, occasionally
eyeing Eloise Joiner with open curiosity. A reporter
from the *Tattler* took notes. The story in Mr. Burch's
paper would probably not allude to any other case
before Judge Boardman.

The judge then instructed the jury. They must ignore anything about a divorce action or testimony
therein. The verdict would be either innocent or
guilty of grand larceny, a felony.

The courtroom then cleared as the weary sun was
settling on the ridge in the southwest. Lytell gathered Daniel, Hannah, and Eloise Joiner and took
them across the courthouse square to the Cattle-
men's Hotel for dinner. He had nothing to say.
Daniel looked drawn and grim. Hannah squeezed
his hand, and he returned the pressure. This would

probably be their last meal together, their last moments in unison. She longed to hug him, to let her tears flow over his cheek.

Eloise made conversation. "They wouldn't let me talk. They wouldn't let you defend yourself. This isn't justice. Whatever happens, I'm going to tell the story to people. They won't shut me up!"

They were summoned back by a messenger barely after they had finished, and they filed into the lamplit courtroom where the court and jury had already assembled.

"Have you come to a verdict?" Boardman asked.

"We have."

"How find you?"

"Guilty as charged, Your Honor."

Chapter 34

The wintry morning light filtered into the Archuleta County courtroom, but Amos Burch thought it was no match for the darkness within him. Beside him, on a spectator bench, sat the bank's attorney, Mark St. John. Several rows behind him sat the postmaster, Horatio Bates, always a spectator at these events.

Nearby sat Hannah Knott, looking pale and taut. Beside her sat Eloise Joiner, her lips compressed, wearing black as if she were about to attend a funeral. Which in fact was just about correct.

A man's life was being taken from him.

During the sentencing, Judge Boardman peered over his gold-rimmed spectacles at the defendant, whose able attorney stood beside him. The prosecutor, Erich Braunfels, stood apart.

"Daniel Knott, you are herewith sentenced to fifteen years imprisonment for your embezzlement.

That is the maximum the law allows. I have done this because of your egregious, heinous, offensive defense, in which you attempted to tar Amos Burch with the crime you committed. I can scarcely express my indignation and revulsion at your effort to turn this town's moral and spiritual preceptor into a forger. The man is not capable of it, as the jury well knew."

Knott seemed to wilt under the rebuke, but then straightened himself and stood, alone, without help or hope. His eyes had turned into great pits of darkness.

"Have you anything to say?"

"Yes, sir. I was never allowed to make my defense. I am innocent."

The judge snorted.

Several persons snickered. Boardman did not stop them.

"A jury of your peers found otherwise. Now, about another matter: the bank's suit against you to recover what was stolen. Upon finding that you are guilty as charged, I am entering a summary judgment in favor of the Merchant Bank to attach all your assets. Mrs. Knott is to vacate the house within seven days. Your bank account, now totaling three hundred seven dollars and twelve cents, is also attached. The estimated value of all your property comes to less than half of what you embezzled. It is so ordered."

Hannah Knott clenched her hands. She would be turned into the streets with her children.

Amos Burch watched her and felt the sadness within him flow through his soul. He could not help her; hoped she had relatives.

Eben Lytell addressed the judge: "Your Honor, I beg you to consider this man's record. He has no prior convictions. He is the sole support of his family. I petition the court to reduce his sentence by half, which would be consistent with the sentencing practices of other judges for this offense."

Boardman bristled. "He has no record, but he was placed in a position of fiduciary trust and betrayed the bank, its borrowers, and his employer. He did so over several years, with calculation. No, Mr. Lytell."

Amos Burch felt the weight of his black topcoat on his shoulders, which wrapped him like a shroud.

"Bailiff, allow the defendant to say farewell to his wife for a few minutes, and then take him to Sheriff Kennear, who will arrange for his passage to the Colorado State Penitentiary."

Boardman stood, and Amos rose, as did the others, and then the judge vanished into chambers.

Amos watched Hannah approach Daniel Knott. They hugged wordlessly, almost primly, two devastated people. He was sorry about it, but Knott had brought it upon himself. None of this had needed to happen.

"Well, Amos, that's that. The bank'll get much of it back," St. John said. "Unrepentant devil. I think if Knott had offered some sort of mea culpa, Boardman would have relented a little. But that Knott's the oddest fellow I've ever met."

"He's a man of honor," Burch said.

"That's an odd comment to make about a man bent on destroying your reputation, Amos. This also means you've defeated Myrtle," St. John continued. "Alden has only to argue that Knott's testimony has been impeached by his conviction. I think you'll be able to put that in your past. There's the jury, of course. They heard a little of it, but Braunfels did his best to stop it. There's Mrs. Joiner's sensations, of course, but now she's an admitted liar and that won't get anywhere."

"Let's go," Amos said. His feet felt like lead.

"Congratulations, Amos," said Horatio Bates. Then, upon noting Amos's ashen face, he hastened to add, "or should I not congratulate you?"

"There is no pleasure in this day," Amos said.

"I am not easy with this," said Bates.

"Then you're the only one in town," St. John said proudly.

"Why would a proper young man do it?"

"Mr. Bates, the mail awaits your attention."

"Stagecoach arrives at ten-thirty," Bates retorted.

Burch ignored him. He abandoned St. John on the boardwalk and walked slowly to the Merchant Bank, thinking about nothing, not wanting to think at all.

The town slumbered in the weak sun, innocent and yearning for its own perfection. He had saved it. Myrtle's scandalous divorce action lay buried. He could remain the exemplar of right conduct. He could continue to lead prayers, give commencement addresses, make sure the right people served in office, offer charity to the unfortunate, and guide business toward high ground. He and Myrtle would eventually pass on and be buried in the small mausoleum he had constructed at the Bethany Cemetery just up the valley. For his epitaph he had chosen the words—and already had them incised in the granite—"Born to Serve."

He entered the bank, nodded curtly to Pickering, avoided the gaze of Miss Gustafson, and plunged into his office. He closed the door, shutting out Paradise.

The morning's *Tattler* lay on his desk.

KNOTT CONVICTED That was the headline. He didn't bother with the story. It would not mention the allusions to a divorce case that once or twice had threatened to escape the tight confines of the courtroom, something that Prescott Boardman unceremoniously stuffed back into the box.

Why had he done it? How had he violated everything he ever stood for? Why was he willing to crush another person for the simple virtue of sticking to the truth? He could not fathom his own conduct. The simpleminded would say it was to save face, but that was nonsense. This tragic violation of his own sacred ideals was rooted in things more complex. He ached to understand, but somehow the explanation of his own aberrant conduct eluded him. He knew only that we strive for our own perfection, but keep falling away from it, and then strive once more, only to fail again.

Daniel Knott was a sterling man, a hero, a man with moral courage and vision. He had sacrificed everything to do what, in his heart of hearts, he knew was right. He was ten times the man that Amos Burch would ever be. Perhaps it was poetic that a truly honorable man would be sentenced to prison, his name blackened forever. Truly heroic men didn't belong, had no claim to the earth. Men like Daniel Knott were so radical, so towering, that the world could not bear to have them around, upsetting everything, destroying all the small, smooth compromises that were the fabric of civilized life. So Daniel Knott had to be put away and broken, and released only after memory had faded.

Burch had feet of clay, and he belonged. Paradise was his home. He was comfortable among its businessmen. He played small-stakes poker with his friends the county officials. His suggestions turned into county ordinances, and these were so fair, so exemplary, that Archuleta County was the model in Colorado for enlightened government.

Yes, he belonged. Knott never would.

He simply could not fathom why he had behaved contrary to everything he held sacred. Had the devil taken him? If only he had swiftly confessed his liaison with Eloise. That would have been understood and forgotten. If only he had granted poor Myrtle her well-deserved divorce. That, too, would have swiftly passed out of mind in Paradise, for no mortal is perfect, and no mortal goes through life without wronging others, no matter how hard one tries.

He was beyond explaining. It would have been so simple to acknowledge his failings. His stature among his fellow citizens would not even have been diminished. But something had caused him to dig himself deeper and deeper into a pit from which he could no longer escape.

He withdrew a pad of foolscap, plucked up his nib pen, and uncorked the ink bottle. He would write the confession in full. But then he decided that a duplicate ought to be made as well, because there were those in town with their own agendas who might hide his confession from the public eye.

"I, Amos C. Burch, herewith confess certain crimes and failings, committed against my beloved wife, Myrtle, against my employee, Daniel Knott, against the justice system of this county, and against Almighty God . . ."

He penned the whole story, scratching out words, blotting mistakes, rewriting his document and then copying it carefully. He did not spare himself. He made certain that Prescott Boardman would read his confession and release Daniel Knott immediately and restore his possessions to him.

He wrote a last sentence apologizing to Knott for stealing his honor and his good name. For Daniel Knott was a hero.

Then, as a footnote, he wrote that two copies of his confession existed, one of them en route to a certain public official in Denver, with explicit instructions that would ensure that it be made public.

He signed each confession. To the one that would

be found on his desk, he added Knott's innocent and accurate ledger pages, which had lain in a folder in his desk all the while, invisible because, as Lytell has surmised, they were in plain sight of everyone.

It was late in the afternoon by the time he had finished with his work. Pickering was closing the accounts. The bank doors had been locked for an hour.

Burch left the bank, envelope in hand, and walked to the post office through the early darkness of the new year. He dropped the letter into the brass-bound mail slot, consigning it to Horatio Bates's care, and returned to the darkened bank. His key scraped in the lock and he walked among haunting shadows to his refuge.

Alone at last.

He settled in his swivel chair and pondered his life. He felt cold. Perhaps it was nothing more than the dying fires in the bank's stoves. He had failed. He might have succeeded by the simple act of confessing his sin. The world was ever forgiving. What had his walk upon this earth come to? Ashes.

Myrtle would have her separation from him and a comfortable income for life. Knott would be acclaimed as a future model for youth, everything that Burch was not.

His lawyers would be cleared. He had never once revealed his designs to them, but had used them to further his schemes. The outside auditors would be cleared. He had never told them of his deception. As for Eloise, he explained in his confession that he had coerced and coached her into the false deposition, using his financial hold on her and her fear of losing her reputation.

Eloise would be taken care of. She had found the courage to pull free of him, and he admired her for it. She was a grand woman who would make a place for herself in a harsh world. She had turned a hard-luck childhood into a great, gritty courage.

He wondered whether he had done everything properly, leaving no loose ends. Knott wasn't scheduled to be taken to the penitentiary until the following week. Now he would never make that trip.

He settled in his chair and addressed God: "You will have to deal with a man who went wrong," he said. "I will never understand my own conduct. But I am sorry."

That was all. He reached into his drawer, removed the cold revolver, and steeled himself to leave Paradise forever.

Chapter 35

Fifteen years of this. Was it worth it? All Knott got out of it was a clear conscience, and even that was little comfort. Had he betrayed his wife and children? Was his love of them less important than telling the exact truth?

He huddled under a thin blanket all night, knowing that he faced endless years of sheer cold unless they paroled him. Then dawn came, followed by a sodden bowl of oatmeal brought by a deputy, and then Sheriff Kennear. Oddly the man was smiling.

"Knott. I'm taking you to court."

"Will you let me wash up?"

"I don't think you'll want to."

"What is this about?"

"You'll see."

It would probably be something more to pile on his broken heart.

Kennear led him upstairs, down a hall, and into

the courtroom where his fate had been sealed the previous day.

The brightness of the morning sun half blinded him. Judge Boardman peered down at him from his perch. Eben Lytell wasn't present. The prosecutor, Erich Braunfels, was, however, and was looking dour. So this would be something still worse, if that were possible.

Knott summoned his courage and stood tall before the judge, determined not to surrender his dignity.

"We're releasing you," Boardman said, without preamble.

"On bail?"

"No, you're a free man. I've vacated the sentence."

Knott blinked, disbelieving.

"Mr. Braunfels here disapproves, but I have so ordered it. He wants to keep you down there until he completes a thorough investigation. But you're free to walk through those doors."

Knott couldn't fathom it. The sunlight struck motes in the quiet courtroom. He saw only a bailiff and the clerk.

Boardman sighed. "How little the court knew. Your defense, which I considered immaterial—'preposterous' is the word—turned out to be true in every respect." The judge cleared his throat. "Amos Burch killed himself last night and left a detailed confession, along with your original ledgers."

"Killed himself?" The news struck Knott like a fist in the belly.

"Yes, with his revolver, no doubt about it. Who would have thought it? I'll never understand it," Boardman said. "But in a way I do. Amos reached high. Sometimes we reach too high and betray the very things we reach for."

"He's dead? Because of me?"

"Not because of you. He wove his own fate."

A tidal wave of feeling flooded through Knott. Pity, resentment at Burch, bitterness, and sorrow that a once-good man had destroyed himself.

"You're exonerated. Everything you said was true." The judge nodded toward Braunfels. "Because the divorce proceedings were sealed, he knew nothing of your testimony in that matter. But when Eloise Joiner testified yesterday morning, I began to wonder."

Knott barely heard the judge's drone.

"I'll bring Eloise Joiner in and scold her. Because of her false swearing, injustice befell you. But I'll let her go. She was under duress. Amos Burch was a powerful man with an iron hand that held the key to her ranch.

"You're a brave and honorable man, Mr. Knott, sticking to the truth like that. In the end, you proved to be stronger than this town's preceptor. We can only pity him, but we can honor you as a great American and an example for all the world to see."

Knott swallowed back the bile in his throat.

"Thank you, sir."

"I'm not done. I'm vacating my judgment against you in the civil suit. Your funds in the bank, your home and possessions, all are restored to you. I'll notify Mark St. John at once. I want to make you whole again."

Knott knew that nothing the court could do would make him whole. But he nodded.

Boardman turned to the sheriff. "Mr. Kennear, do the paperwork and let him go."

The sheriff nodded.

"Your Honor, what happened? Amos Burch is dead? I still don't understand," Knott said.

Boardman spoke gently. "Yesterday afternoon, Amos shut himself in his office and wrote two copies of this confession—which you're free to read, if you wish—laying the entire burden on himself. Apparently after the bank was closed he crossed the street and mailed one copy of his confession to someone. Then he returned to his office and sometime early in the evening, shot himself. This morning Miss Gustafson found him, and fled the bank to report the matter to Sheriff Kennear. By nine o'clock this confession, along with the ledgers, were in my hands.

"The first thing I did after reading Burch's document was compare the forged ledgers to yours. And yes, suddenly that capital *M* meant everything, corroborating Burch's admissions. He had slipped up, writing that *M*. . . ."

Boardman shook his head, stood, walked around

his desk, descended from the dais, and clasped Knott's hand.

"Not one in a thousand, not one in *ten* thousand . . ." he said. And Daniel Knott smiled for the first time in eons.

"Go greet your wife and children," Boardman said. "You'll be hearing from Myrtle Burch in a while. She never expected her marriage to end in this fashion. She's grieving now. She loved Amos even if he turned her love aside. But she told me when we spoke earlier how indebted she is to you. Paradise is indebted to you."

Knott thanked the judge and returned to his cell, bewildered.

Amos Burch, dead. The man who had wrecked a life, a family, was dead. The anger that suffused Knott's soul and body would not swiftly dissolve. He knew it would be a long time before he flushed the bitterness out of him. The very mention of Burch would stir up sour memories for a long time. He wished it could be otherwise; wished that he could swiftly forgive and forget. But he knew he was an imperfect mortal in an imperfect world, and that healing would take years.

Kinnear handed him his street clothes. He felt a desperate need to shave before seeing Hannah; to walk into her arms restored in every way and not looking like a jailbird. But he couldn't stand that dark place one moment more.

"You gonna clean up?" Kennear asked.

"No, I'm going to get out."

"I'm glad you're not stuck here, Dan."

"So am I!"

They laughed.

He walked through a mild morning, bathed in sunlight. Going home.

Hannah screamed when she saw him. "You've got to go back!" she cried. "If they catch you—"

"Hannah, Hannah . . ."

He had walked into the quiet house and found her packing the children's small treasures.

She gasped, couldn't seem to swallow, and then reeled into his arms. He held her, felt her arms clutch at him, felt her hair brush his face, heard her convulsive sobs.

"Hannah, I'm free. They let me go."

"No, it can't be."

"Amos Burch killed himself last night," he said, his hands drawing his wife tight. "He left a confession."

"Oh, Daniel. He died?"

"I'm sorry it happened."

"But why?"

"Because Amos Burch was a good man. He couldn't bear his own guilt. He was—a man filled with ideas, disappointed in himself. So disappointed that he pulled the trigger. But he wrote it all out, tried to make things right."

"They'll never be right, Daniel."

"Yes, but we don't have to move. Judge Boardman gave us everything back. This is our home again."

"Oh, God, Daniel." Tears swept her cheeks.

"We can tell the children their father's an innocent man," he said, touching on one of the most painful things he had endured.

"Yes! We'll tell Rosalie! She's outside somewhere."

She abandoned the packing, and they walked slowly down the stairs to the parlor and sat side by side on the sofa. Neither spoke. The sun played coyly with the lace curtains, but there were long shadows in the room. It was all too much to grasp. For weeks, they had been ruled by desperation. For weeks, they had been pariahs in Paradise. Now, suddenly, it had all changed. Daniel knew, though, that some would still blame him for Amos Burch's death, and squint at him with malice. It would never be over.

"Tell me the rest," she said.

He told her how it had all happened. That Myrtle's divorce suit had come to a shocking end; that Judge Boardman would deal sternly with Eloise Joiner but still let her go.

"I'm glad of that," Hannah said.

"Hannah . . . there's always going to be something between us. I don't know if it'll ever go away."

"Yes," she said.

"I'll put words to it. You'll always believe I put my family, you and my children, second. That this was an act of disloyalty."

"I know you were torn, Dan."

"I have no answer for you. I did what I had to do. I want to think that somehow, in the far beyond, what I did *was* loyal to you. I know I caused suffering, to Rosalie especially. And to you, too. Because I didn't bend, you lived in shame and the boys and Rosalie were cruelly treated. Hannah, my only reply is that maybe I set a good example. Everything did work out."

She didn't respond, and he knew he had touched the pain that lay dark and forbidding within her. He didn't know how he could heal his children. Just telling them their father was no crook wouldn't be enough. Those taunts and slights and stones would haunt them all their lives unless he could somehow heal them. He had no such gifts or powers.

What had virtue wrought? Was it worth it?

Their future would not be easy.

Chapter 36

Myrtle Burch, who suddenly found herself the principal stockholder of the bank, a director, and its chief officer, offered Knott a position as president, with the board's approval. He thought about it and declined.

"Well, Daniel," she said. "We're disappointed. But count on me for a recommendation. I will endorse you anytime, anywhere, for any position you choose."

"You are kind," he said. "We hope to move soon."

"Paradise isn't suitable?"

"Too many memories and hurts."

"I'm sorry. I feel somewhat responsible."

"Mrs. Burch, nothing you did caused any of this."

"Well, I'm not staying either. I'm going to Hartford as soon as the estate's settled. We're both weary of Paradise."

He nodded. He didn't want to live in any sort of

earthly paradise. He wanted to live where people didn't aspire to change human nature into something more lofty than it ever could be.

One good thing came of it all: Daniel stopped regretting his stubborn honesty. He had done the right thing. He had not been disloyal or unloving to his family. In fact, his truthfulness under pressure had been a form of loyalty to them, and to the ideals of the community and the country to which he had been born.

The mayor and assorted ministers pleaded with him to address banquets or lead prayers, all for the good of the children.

"You're our George Washington," said one. "He would not tell a lie, and neither would you."

"Well, thank you, but I didn't do anything special. I did what any good citizen would do."

He turned down numerous offers, until at last the leaders of Paradise stopped asking.

But Horatio Bates had other notions. He corralled Knott one day during a slack hour at the post office and thrust a cup of steaming java at him.

"I want to hear the whole story. You're one of a kind, Daniel," he said.

Reluctantly—though Bates alone had gingerly supported him through his ordeal—Knott described the pressures on him, his anguish, the questioning even by his family, and his ultimate vindication.

"You're a hero whether you agree or not," Bates said. "And I'll tell you why: because love demanded that you spare your family the pain. But you went ahead, knowing that there's a larger love. Once your children grow past all this, they'll be filled with unspeakable pride, and they'll go into the world armed and ready to be just as upright themselves."

Knott had grown used to this sort of acclaim, and now he didn't resist it as he had at first.

"I've been pondering this," Bates said. "That's what village philosophers—and maybe village idiots—like to do. The ideals that inspired Amos Burch can be found all over the West, in most every frontier town. A new land! A beginning! A chance to reach for perfection. Oh, I've seen it wherever I've sorted mail. People have the sense that everything can be remade, and that if only we apply enough wisdom, enough character, enough courage, we can fashion something unheard of in the annals of history—a near-perfect world.

"I once asked Amos Burch why the town was called Paradise. I expected the usual reply. A handsome setting, a virgin land, majestic mountains, glowing and verdant valleys, sweet rushing rivers, safety . . . but he never mentioned any of that. He told me it's because this haven is the place to make the world new, and to take what we've learned back East and cure the corruption back there. Like ascending to heaven and passing through the pearlies, and entering a city with golden streets and ivory, and alabaster, and perpetual sun. Like that, Daniel. Perfection, paradise on earth."

"I've never heard anything like that in my years here."

"No, of course not. It's implied, never quite expressed because we all know that man is a fallen creature, and it's only a dream. But I've listened to the undertone, the distant harmonies on the ridges, the leitmotif, and I hear it in the talk of this town, in Amos Burch's words of wisdom, in the lofty sermons of our divines—I hear that music of the spheres."

Knott didn't know what all that had to do with Burch's vicious assault on him, or what he had suffered, or even why he felt so restless in Paradise.

"Seems more like old-fashioned pride to me, Horatio. The man couldn't bear to have his carnal sin exposed, after setting himself up as a local saint."

"Well, yes. That, too."

"That was all there was to it."

The postmaster smiled and disagreed. "I collect heroes, you know. Some pass through physical danger. Some pass through temptation and spiritual danger. Most heroes are wounded along the way. You certainly were gravely wounded, along with those you love. But that is one of the signs of heroism. In spite of your wounds, you did what was right. In spite of the bleeding of your soul, you stood tall until they knocked you down, and then stood tall again because no earthly power could make you lie or violate what was sacred within you." He reached out to touch Knott. "Someday I'm going to write these notions up."

"You do that, Horatio. But leave me out of it."

Knott was growing uncomfortable. He grinned, patted the postmaster on the shoulder, and slid out into the sunlight. He was growing more at ease by the day, and so were those who had shunned him. On the street he now met smiles instead of frowns or averted eyes.

But the wounds remained.

He didn't know where to go. His funds, accumulated during his brief palmy days as the bank's chief officer, were dwindling from his account.

The most tangled and painful part of all this was Hannah. Sometimes she seemed distant, other times almost tearful. Occasionally tender and open to him. He knew why: she still felt betrayed.

Then, one night, long after the children had fallen asleep, she stirred in their bed, found the hollow of his shoulder, and snuggled into it. He knew she was weeping. He held her gently, not knowing whether she would throw his arm off.

"I love you more than I ever have," she said. "I love you because you're a man of honor, a man I can always trust, an example for our children. I love you because you're you, and not anyone lesser or weaker."

"Hannah . . ."

"I want to renew my vows. I love you for better, for worse, for richer, for poorer, in sickness and in health. I almost failed, but I will never fail again."

"You didn't fail. I probably did."

"No! You didn't!"

"I know why your heart broke."

"Oh, Daniel, it was all because of the pressure. The weight they put on you. You didn't break in two. Oh, Daniel . . ."

"Yes, they put some weight on me," he whispered.

"I'm so glad, Daniel. I'm so glad . . . I love you to the end of time. I'll love you longer than the mountains will stand. I love you because you are the lilac bloom, the sunrise, the sacred place . . ."

"Hannah, oh, Hannah. How I've always loved you, above all else. More than life."

She drifted to sleep after a while, and he knew things would eventually be all right. She had worked her way through the hurt, and now they would be united again. The children were doing better, too. Each child had been honored at school, and teachers had drawn the right lessons, and taught their classes about judgment, persecution, honor, and courage, and about being an American, as well as the value of truth. A lot of rascal boys had learned a few things from their teachers as a result of the Knott family's ordeal. So the good things were spreading outward, like ripples on the pond. And, apart from a few skeptics, Paradise had profited.

Just as, in the end, Hannah and Peter and Daniel Junior and Rosalie had profited in ways too mysterious to reason out.

Something important had happened there in the hush and sacredness of their marital bed. No long explanations; just a renewal of holy bonds. They were again husband and wife, two mortals become one.

Daniel pondered his next step there in the velvety dark. He wanted to pluck up his family and carry it safely to some new place. Not far away. They all loved Colorado, and the frontier, and the feeling that they were in a fresh, sweet, new world that beckoned to mortals like themselves.

There were so many banks, and he now had a pocketful of recommendations. Fairplay, Leadville, Ouray, Silverton, Telluride, Durango. He thought to try banking in a mining town, where people weren't filled with visions of paradise. Where no Amos Burch, well intentioned but wrestling with human nature, would stamp a town in some utopian fashion. For there were no real utopias and never would be.

But then he corrected himself. There, in the small compass of his marital bed, was his own utopia, and there he found not perfection but unending forgiveness and love and honor.

Tomorrow he would write letters to request interviews for a new job.

RALPH COTTON

"Gun-smoked, blood-stained, gritty
believability...Ralph Cotton writes the sort
of story we all hope to find within us."

—Terry Johnston

"Cotton's blend of history and imagination
works." —*Wild West Magazine*

❏ Misery Express   0-451-19999-5/$5.99

❏ Badlands   0-451-19495-8/$5.99

❏ Justice   0-451-19496-9/$5.99